SALAMANDER
and Other Stories

Masuji Ibuse

KODANSHA INTERNATIONAL LTD.
Tokyo, New York & San Francisco

Originally published by Kodansha International Ltd. under the title *Lieutenant Lookeast and Other Stories* (with one additional story).

Published by Kodansha International Ltd., 12–21 Otowa 2-chome, Bunkyo-ku, Tokyo 112 and Kodansha International/USA Ltd., 10 East 53rd Street, New York, New York 10022 and 44 Montgomery Street, San Francisco, California 94104. Copyright © 1981 by Kodansha International Ltd. All rights reserved. Printed in Japan.

LCC 80–84421
ISBN 0–87011–458–1
JBC 0093–789396–2361

First paperback edition, 1981

CONTENTS

Preface

The work of Masuji Ibuse is an acquired taste; not in the sense that it is difficult to enjoy on first reading, but in the sense that extensive acquaintance with it deepens one's pleasure and understanding of its art.

At eighty-three, Ibuse can look back on a large and varied output, from the 1923 "Salamander" to *Black Rain*, the 1965 novel on Hiroshima, and beyond. Most of it, with the exception of *Black Rain*, consists of pieces of short or medium length—which is one reason, perhaps, why he has been less translated than some other Japanese writers of comparable stature.

The range of themes, as the nine stories in this book show, is wide. There are the early, more consciously literary and intellectual pieces with a strong element of fantasy such as "Salamander." There are semi-autobiographical pieces such as "Carp" (1926). Other comparatively early pieces, of which "Plum Blossom by Night" (1930) is a good example, seem to owe more, both in form and manner, to the European short story.

There is a body of stories on historical themes, represented here by "Yosaku the Settler" (1955). It is a characteristic of these that, while sometimes drawing heavily on documentary sources, they succeed by what appear to be the simplest of means in giving the characters humanity, the setting a sense of actuality, and the theme a universal relevance. The same skill was to serve Ibuse in good stead when, in *Black Rain*, he created a work of art out of a mass of firsthand accounts of the bombing of Hiroshima.

There are many scenes of country life that show, along with a vivid appreciation of the virtues and shortcomings of the Japanese peasant, a vein of gentle humor that is found at its broadest in ''Old Ushitora'' (1950). Occasionally, as in the disturbing story ''Lieutenant Lookeast'' (1950), the humor gives way to biting satire; to read this work is to realize the intensity of feeling that lies behind the gentle mocking of human foibles.

Some works, finally, such as the remarkable "Life at Mr. Tange's" (1931), show a combination of realism and symbolism, broad humor and poetry, realism and fantasy, that display Ibuse's techniques at their most quintessential and defy classification.

Despite the variety of themes, the stories share certain characteristics of technique and manner. There is the absence of extended descriptive passages, of "fine writing" for its own sake. Characters and physical settings are sketched in with a few details that are concrete and particular. Around them, there is space. The effect is to give the characters something of the quality of caricatures, or of actors on a stage: they are simultaneously slightly larger than life and seen at a distance.

The writing is spare. Carefully molded images and fragments of dialogue succeed each other without comment. The mood changes subtly, often abruptly. Effects are built up by setting these varied elements next to each other without unnecessary padding. The impression is of a self-effacement on the part of the author that extends to a dislike of underscoring any point too heavily. The dialogue makes its points slyly; sometimes the motives, even the action itself, are half-concealed.

This dislike of too clearly stated positions is one of the most marked features of the personality that emerges from Ibuse's work. Yet one feels that the ambiguity is not a sign of weakness, but of a conscious distaste for assertive statements, founded in a fullness of experience. Arising from the interaction of elements that are in-

8

trinsically strong, it comes to be felt as constituting, in itself, a positive statement.

The other obvious characteristics of the author's personality are humor and compassion, well-worn if fundamental virtues that are dispensed in a blend peculiar to Ibuse. The humor is often gently mocking, directed now at a particular individual (the hero of "Plum Blossom by Night"), now at intellectual pretension ("Salamander"), now at genteel prudery (the extinguishing of the lamp before the mating of Myōkendō's cow in "Old Ushitora"), now at the author's own person (the writer from Tokyo, also in "Old Ushitora"). At times, as in "Carp," it almost seems a weapon of self-defense against an excess of feeling.

The compassion is sometimes, as in "Yosaku the Settler," implicit in the theme of the story. But it is at its subtlest and most effective when it combines with humor, as in the passage in "Yosaku" where the thief imagines himself returning one day to die in the imperial tomb that he has helped to rifle, or in Mr. Tange's reminiscences and the arrival of Ei's wife in "Life at Mr. Tange's."

Humor, compassion, a plebeian quality, an absence of sentimentality, a detached, almost satirical view of humanity, abruptness, a subtle poetry, a strong feeling for the Japanese countryside in its unprettified actuality—it is no wonder that some Japanese critics have pointed out a similarity between Ibuse and Hokusai, especially the Hokusai of the "Thirty-Six Views of Mt. Fuji." And once the resemblance is noted, it is tempting to recall also Hokusai's contemporary, Hiroshige, with his romanticism, sentimentality, lyrical feeling for color, and his greater urbanity, and to see the two artists as representing two opposing aspects of the Japanese character that can be detected in literature as well as in art. Yet whether that parallel can be validly drawn or not, it is certain at least that Ibuse's work has a strength and deep-lying humanity that deserves attention in the West both for its own sake and for the light it throws on the Japanese character.

John Bester

Plum Blossom by Night

Late one night—more precisely, at around two in the morning on February 20 last year—I was driven by an extremely empty stomach and a feeling of boredom to walk the main thoroughfare of the Ushigome Benten district of Tokyo in search of an *oden* restaurant or some other cheap eating place. Within the high wall of a large private house, white plum blossom was in bloom, a pleasing sight as, stopping to turn up the collar of my cloak, I glanced up briefly towards the sky. But just then, quite without warning, the figure of a man came staggering towards me out of the gloom around the foot of a telegraph pole.

"Hey, you!" he shouted, planting himself in my path and sticking his chin out for me to see. "Is there blood on my face?"

The man's words alarmed me greatly. Examining him in the light of a street lamp, I found that he was right. Someone, it seemed, had dealt his right cheek a blow of some force, and the flesh was broken in two places, at the corner of his mouth and below his ear. The blood was spurting rhythmically from the gashes, soaking his collar, and he wiped at it incessantly with the palm of his hand. Like myself, he wore a cloak over his kimono, with a soft hat on his head. He exuded a pronounced odor of drink.

"You're hurt pretty badly, aren't you? Did you get the worst of a quarrel?" I asked, retreating a few paces before putting the question. Something about his bearing towards me suggested a still smoldering excitement that possibly stemmed from a drunken quarrel.

But he grabbed at the flap of my cloak and refused to let go, tugging at it till he threatened to tear it.

"Here, let me go!" I demanded.

"No, I won't!" he said. "I'm thinking of lodging a complaint. I've been beaten up by four or five men from the fire station. I'm going to the police. Be my witness, will you?"

"How can I? I didn't see what happened. I wonder, though, if you didn't do or say something yourself that upset the firemen in the first place?"

"D'you know, I just don't remember anything at all. I was too drunk. Anyway, it's outrageous when you get beaten up by members of the fire brigade, of all people. So you must be my witness!"

"Sorry, it's impossible. What I will testify, though, is that you were badly hurt. There's a police box over there."

The lamp over the police box at Enoki-cho was clearly visible. But he changed his mind.

"The truth is, you know, I live right near here, so I don't want to kick up too much fuss about it. That would make trouble where I work. It hurts, but perhaps I'd better let them off after all."

For a drunk, and a drunk with a grievance at that, he seemed to be showing a considerable fund of good sense. I was moving off, therefore, thinking to leave him to his own devices, when again he took an uncompromising hold of the flap of my cloak.

"You wouldn't go off in such a hurry, would you? Tell me, now—what d'you think I should say to the boss when I get back to the shop? You see, with a face like this he's bound to realize I've had a scrap."

"I suppose so. Show me your face again, then. We may be able to cook up some story."

"Well?" he inquired. "It's pretty bad, I expect?"

He brought his face close to mine, and in the dim light I inspected his wounds with all the assumed composure of a doctor's assistant.

"This is terrible!" With my left hand in the pocket of my cloak, I moved his chin up and down and from side to side with my right.

"I see. . . ." I said. "Now put your chin up a little bit more. I call this a bit much, really! You've been poked in the cheek with a stick or something, haven't you?"

"I've no idea, I was drunk."

"The wound on your mouth, too—it looks as though it's been torn open at the corner. No teeth loose?"

He ran his tongue round his teeth.

"My teeth are all right."

"That's good. Now, when you get home, tell your boss this: you were going home drunk on a streetcar, standing on the step enjoying the breeze, with your hands tucked into your kimono sleeves, when the streetcar suddenly rounded a curve and you were shaken off head first. And you were unlucky enough to strike your cheek on an upturned paving stone."

"I see. Yes—that's what I'll tell him!"

"I must say, your face is a bit too damaged even for that, which is awkward. But still, he may swallow it if you lay it on thick enough."

I took my hand away from his chin.

"Two things you'll have to keep reminding him of," I added. "First, that you fell with your chin down, and second that you were, after all, drunk."

"Right you are! Thanks! You're a great fellow." He puffed out his cheeks, expelled the air, staggered, and spat.

"Well, I'm off," I said, making to take my leave.

"So soon? Now, I call that unfriendly!"

He lunged after me, and I thought he was going to insist on our taking a walk together. But he thrust out his right hand instead.

Assuming that, as always with drunks, he wanted to shake hands, I stretched out my own hand, to receive not a handshake but something remarkably like a coin that he seemed to be trying to press into my palm. As I drew my hand back in a reflex movement, there came the unmistakable sound of a coin falling to the ground. Holding on to my cloak with one hand, with the other he picked up the object that had fallen onto the ground in the dark and held it up in the light of the lamp.

"Damn!" he said. "A *copper* coin." Hastily, he tucked the coin away in the pocket of his cloak and fetched out something else.

Conscious of the smile spreading over my face, I brushed aside his arm in an attempt to make my escape, whereupon he suddenly thrust whatever he was holding into my cloak pocket. Taking it out, I found it was a five-yen note.

"You were trying to give me this, weren't you?" I said. "Well, you're not going to. Here. . . ."

I placed it on the brim of the soft hat he was wearing and tried to flee. But he had a firm grasp on the flap of my cloak. Abruptly, he started to prod me in the chest.

"Hey, that's enough!" I cried. "What d'you think you're . . . ?"

"It's because you won't take it. You're too big for your boots. If you don't take it, I'll tell people *you* did this to my face."

He set about throttling me, with every sign of confidence in his own skill.

"Wait!" Somehow, I had to calm him down. "Wait! I'll take it."

"Take it, then! If you think you're going to make a fool of me. . . ."

"I'll come and get it tomorrow morning."

"Oh no you won't! Here we go again, then!"

"Cut out the rough stuff! Let me go and I'll take it."

He picked up the note, which had fallen to the ground, and, putting it in my pocket, leaped away from me and assumed a posture that warned he would hit out if I came any nearer.

"All right, then," I said. "Let's do it like this: tomorrow morning, I'll drop by with a box of cakes or something and inquire how you're doing. That way I shall see your boss, and I can say to him, this is nothing special but here you are, this is for your injured employee. And while I'm about it, I can tell him the story about the streetcar too."

14

"Now, there's a good idea!" He relaxed his aggressive posture in favor of his former drunken stance.

"You'd better give me your name and address, then," I said.

He replied in an unsteady voice, still keeping a wary distance. "Jūkichi Murayama, care of Ishikawa, 37 Tsurumaki-cho."

I committed what he said to memory, my fingers all the while busily folding and refolding the note inside my pocket.

"Care of Ishikawa, Jūkichi Murayama, right? Number thirty-seven. Care of Ishikawa, Jūkichi Murayama. . . ."

"Right. . . . Right. Don't forget the box of cakes, now. Tell him to give them to the head clerk."

"Don't you worry. Care of Ishikawa, right?"

He walked unsteadily away, apparently satisfied. The five-yen note was beginning to bother me even more than if I had, say, found it on the street and pocketed it. It worried me so much, in fact, that I gave up my search for an *oden* shop.

Early the next morning, while I was still asleep, I received a visit from a friend of my university days, a man called Yasuo Tawa who worked in the broker's section of the Yamagano Trading Company. He had had a windfall a few days before, he said, and was going to take me out for a meal. So eager was he to get me out with him, in fact, that he could barely restrain his impatience while I washed. So we went to the Beniya, in the Kagurazaka quarter, where he plied me with one thing after another.

Two or three times a month, Tawa would come to see me and talk a great deal, mostly about fluctuations in the market. He disapproved heartily of the way I went from printing house to printing house, doing proofreading on a piecework basis.

"It's no good carrying on like an odd-job man at everyone's beck and call," he said. "The actual work you do doesn't matter, of course, but you mustn't let yourself get stale. You must project yourself more into the future. Be more positive, that's what I say!"

On one occasion, he even produced a woman's silk jacket with a red lining, which he hung inside out on the hat rack in my room, insisting that it would make me feel, at least, a bit more positive.

"It's easy for you to talk, telling me to be more positive," I said, "but one just can't do it all in a rush."

"You let the world bully you, that's the trouble," he said. "I'm going to put some new life into you. You've got to be more positive, now."

But he never did succeed in effecting the change.

On leaving the Beniya, we went back to my place and talked until late at night. As a result, I failed to call on Jūkichi Murayama as I had promised. Instead, I took the opportunity while Tawa was reading the evening paper to send a letter by special delivery.

"Dear Mr. Murayama," I wrote, "I fully intended to come to see you this morning, as I was worried about your injuries, but urgent business arose due to an unexpected call from a friend, so I am writing to inquire after you instead. The market these days fluctuates dreadfully, you see. In fact, I am still discussing various things with my friend at the moment. I hope you will forgive me. Where last night's business is concerned, I can't help feeling it was the conductor's fault. In the first place, since you were obviously drunk, he should have kept a more careful eye on you. He should, at the very least, have given you a word of warning before the streetcar went round the curve. As it was, there you were with your hands tucked in your sleeves, taking the air on the steps, when the car suddenly went round a corner. Naturally enough, you fell head first—and there, to add to your bad luck, were the paving stones all up, with the result that you hurt your cheek and mouth badly. Leaping from the streetcar in alarm, I took you up in my arms and inquired your name and address. But the conductor—I wonder how anyone could be so heartless? You might well have killed yourself on that stone, but he made no move at all to stop the car. I myself would take such inhuman conduct to the courts. However, what disturbs me most of all at the moment is the danger that your wounds will become infected. Please take every care, so that you are restored to health just as soon as possible. I ought to come and see you tomorrow, I feel, but, as I already said, the need to see my friend about the market and various other things will keep me busy for some while to come. I hope you will not think badly of me. As soon as I have a moment to spare, I will call without fail to inquire after you. Whatever happens, though, I sincerely hope that you will be completely recovered in the very near future."

I omitted my own name and address. If the truth be told, cigarettes, envelopes, repairs to a wooden clog, and that evening's dinner had made considerable inroads into the five yen of the previous night, and I was not entirely my own master. The idea of that five-yen note and the box of cakes troubled me even more than if I had committed theft. As a child, I once stole an offering from in front of a Buddhist altar in order to buy fishhooks, but even that had not bothered me quite so much as this.

Five or six months passed.

The twenty-sixth of every month was payday and I found myself with a little money in hand. On the twenty-sixth, therefore, I would promptly insert the cleanest five-yen note I could find into the writing-brush stand on my desk, ready to return it to Murayama at any time. This had the effect of preventing any muddle in my finances on account of the five yen; an added advantage was that I did not actually need to return the money, or to call on him, in order to preserve my peace of mind.

Unfortunately, I failed to keep the money by me constantly. On the tenth of every month, I was obliged to pay my board for the last month but one. This meant that during the sixteen days remaining until the afternoon of the twenty-sixth, I could not even board a streetcar without fretting lest I should not have the fare. And so, finally, I would find myself forced to lay hands on the five yen in the brush stand that I had set aside for paying back Murayama.

For a whole year or so, I was forever putting a note in the brush stand or taking it out and spending it. While it was in there I felt no pangs of guilt at all, but at times when I had taken the liberty of borrowing it, I went in terror of meeting Murayama. Who could tell when he might come up from behind and sieze me by the scruff of the neck?

Why, then, if I was so worried, did I not pay this Murayama his five yen and have done with it? The answer is that for people living my kind of life there are two sorts of debt. The amounts involved may be the same, but there is a sort that can be paid back and a sort that cannot. And the debt I owed Murayama quite obviously belonged to the second category. At the same time, though, it was the kind of debt that was a constant worry until one did in fact pay it back.

Worst of all, Jūkichi Murayama appeared to be the kind of man with a violent disposition who must never be allowed to find one off one's guard. Who knew when he might dart out from the shadows without warning and plant himself in my path with a "Hey, you! Is there blood on my face?"

The wall of that large house in Benten-cho, with the white plum blossom spilling over it, rose before my eyes. He grabbed hold of me and refused to let me go. I was supposed to have the money ready for paying back at any time; but that day I did not have five yen to my name. . . . Time and again, as I was walking through the dark streets at night, the imagined scene would send shivers running down my spine.

The plum had bloomed once more this year; already the flowers were beginning to fall. The old tree that stretched its branches over the high wall of the house in Benten-cho had made a fine showing.

One day—not payday, but a day when I had not a penny left save the five-yen note in the brush stand—I determined that I would call on Murayama. Even the plum blossom, you see, seemed to be proclaiming my five-yen fraud. I felt certain that Murayama would be there, staggering beneath that plum tree, and with hands all bloody would stroke my cheek or even, per- haps, try to strangle me. One night, in a public latrine at Iidabashi, I actually thought I felt him doing it. I even came to feel that I had seen an account of the affair, in excessively small print, reported in a recent newspaper.

I located Jūkichi Murayama's home, care of Ishikawa, 37 Tsurumaki-cho, without difficulty. It was the Ishikawa Pawnshop. It was this pawnshop, it seemed, of which he had said he was "head clerk."

Just as I was ducking beneath the short curtain that hung over the doorway—a dark blue curtain, with the legend "Pawnshop" picked out in white—a very convenient way of handling my visit occurred to me. All I needed to do was pretend that I had come to pawn my cloak, give a brief, fictional explanation of my delay on the lines of last year's letter, and return him the five yen. And if he should have sufficiently bad taste to be impressed by the way I took off my cloak, he might well let me pawn it for around ten yen. I was still wearing the same cloak as the previous year.

"Good morning!" I said, undoing the buttons of my cloak. "I'd like to pawn this."

But Jūkichi Murayama was not at the counter; it was a fat, middle-aged man. He was in the act of photographing a camellia in a vase on the shelf, using an old-fashioned camera that someone had doubtless pawned.

Taking my cloak from me with a supercilious air, he turned it inside out, measured the length, and finally made a face as though bothered by the worn places at the back of the neck and the hem.

"Would this be your first time here?" he asked.

"Yes, indeed." I took out my personal seal ready to stamp the necessary form.

"How much would you . . .?"

"Ten yen."

"Ten yen? I'm afraid I can't give you that much."

"Don't worry—I'll redeem it all right."

"But I mean, look how worn the hem and collar are! Imitation melton just doesn't wear well, does it?"

He had both ears stuffed with cotton. It disposed me to feel a mild contempt for him.

"It's *my* cloak until I decide to pawn it, so I'll trouble you to stop insulting it."

"But ten yen, I ask you!"

"And besides, I'm on good terms with your clerk, Jūkichi Murayama, so it's ten yen or nothing!"

"Him? He left here ages ago."

"Gone? Where is he, then?"

"How should I know? Knowing him, I'm quite sure he's up to all kinds of tricks."

Jūkichi Murayama, he told me, had not come home that night last year when he had met me. He had vanished, along with the money kept in hand for buying pawned articles.

In the end I got ten yen for my cloak, with my watch thrown in as well.

Whatever happened now, I felt, I had nothing to fear from Jūkichi Murayama. Why, he was even more clearly a criminal than myself! It was I, in fact, who had had a windfall. I went to the Beniya in Kagurazaka and rang Tawa at the Yamagano Trading Company. He was out. My scheme, if he had been in, had been to summon him, tell him—as he was always so fond of boasting to me—that I had had a windfall in the past two or three days, and propose to stand him drinks and a meal. After all, I must be more positive!

To get things going, I went upstairs to have a coffee and a bowl of sweetened red beans. Resting my feet, shod in the restaurant's slippers, on the gas fire in the corner, I forgot all about Jūkichi Murayama and set about watching the comings and goings of the patrons and waitresses. The waitresses there have smartened up remarkably in recent years.

Leaving there, I went to a Western-style restaurant near Edogawa Bridge. By now the lights were on, and though it was still early the waitresses, their faces heavily coated with white powder, were already drunk. As they went about refilling people's glasses with drink, each of them puffed at a cigarette filched from one or the other of the customers. One of them, with yellow-stained teeth, was plucking at a two-stringed instrument with the self-satisfied air of one who fancies her touch.

From there I went on to another restaurant of the same kind, although I was already drunk.

Finding a seat among the unfamiliar faces, I gazed at my surroundings as I drank. I was much taken with four posters pasted on the walls and glass doors, for on three of the four were splendid life-size pictures of beautiful girls with their hair in the "earphone" style, all of them looking at me and smiling merrily. In their hands, moreover, they held foaming glasses of beer, which they proffered to me. The remaining poster of the four, another beer advertisement, had a picture of a clown on it. He wore peculiar clothes and was smiling with his face screwed up in a grimace. I felt well disposed towards him, however, for he was clearly not mocking me for being tipsy on cheap liquor. He was a merry fellow; in the end, I even found myself smiling too.

Leaving that place considerably under the weather, I entered yet another establishment of the same type. More precisely, I staggered in.

"The drunker I get, the better I carry my drink," I muttered to myself as I staggered to a seat. I sat down, and gave my order.

The place was full of people, the whole lot of them drunk. In places like that, the drunker you are, the more you can throw your weight about. It's fun, and it gives you the feeling that people are kindly disposed to you. What pleasure could be more exquisite? I got so drunk that I stubbed out a cigarette in a plate of soup that I'd just ordered.

"I'm the drunkest man in Tokyo! But the drunker I get, the better I carry my drink," I bawled as I left, reeling in imminent danger of losing my balance. The fronts of the shops lining the street were all shut, and the irregular clip-clop of my wooden clogs echoed like someone kicking the bottom of a wooden tub. There was a cold breeze. Perhaps I had discarded my cloak a little early.

Just then, without warning, a deep voice hailed me as I went past: "Hey, you!"

My heart stopped. The voice from last year—Jūkichi Mura-yama! I stood silent.

I soon realized it came from the police box, but the sight that met my eyes even sooner, as I turned round, was not a police box but the high wall of that residence in Benten-cho. I could actually see the white plum blossom in bloom above my head and the telegraph pole, motionless, directly before my eyes.

Not replying, on tiptoe, I started to make my escape.

"Hey, you!"

I stopped dead in my tracks.

". . . Is there blood on my face?"

With the palm of my hand, I felt the blood on my cheek.

I was the head clerk of the pawnshop.

"Which way are you heading?"

Fence, plum blossom, telegraph pole, vanished all at once. The voice, too, was that of the policeman in his box. Once I realized that, I was not afraid.

"Where are you heading for?"

I made no reply.

"Been quarreling or something?"

I felt my cheek again, but there was no blood, nothing.

"I've no idea, I was drunk."

"You'd better get on home, now."

No reply.

Finally, I fully grasped the fact that I was not Jūkichi Mura-yama; and I satisfied myself that the white plum blossom and the tall fence that I had just seen were products of the illusion that had plagued me throughout the past year. Exultantly—though I reeled in all directions, though I threatened to collapse at any moment or vomit—I made my way home to my lodgings. And I shouted out loud:

"The drunker I get, the better I carry my drink! That bastard Murayama, frightening a fellow! Hey, you, Murayama—you don't scare me! Show yourself, Murayama! Come on now, show yourself!"

Lieutenant Lookeast

In the dialect of our part of the country, anything that disturbs the life of the village is referred to as "ruptions in the village," while anything that upsets one's own small section of the community is called "ruptions over here." "Over here" means one's own particular administrative district of the village, or the people living round about, and "ruptions" is used of anything that disrupts the even tenor of everyday life. In the Sasayama district of our village, we too have our occasional "ruptions over here," which are most annoying to the locals. Their chief source is the peculiar behavior of one Yūichi Okazaki, former lieutenant in the Japanese army.

Yūichi Okazaki, aged thirty two, is not in his right mind. At normal times, he is reasonably well behaved, but labors even so under the delusion that the war is still on and that he himself is a professional soldier just as in former days. Everything he does reproduces, in some way or other, the behavior of a soldier in wartime. At mealtimes, for example, quite without warning, he will draw himself up solemnly at the table and break into a recital of the five-articled Imperial Instructions to the Military: "For the soldier, absolute allegiance. . . ."

Occasionally, when his mother brings home cigarettes she has bought for him, he declares that they are a special imperial gift and, turning towards the east with every sign of intense emotion, makes a profound obeisance. At other times, he will be walking along the street when, quite without warning, he will utter the crisp command "Mark time!" In wartime, when everyone was familiar with such things from seeing the military, all this would have been nothing out of the ordinary, but today it merely seems frivolous. Yūichi, even so, is not really giving orders to others: it is purely for his own satisfaction. If things went no further, in fact, they would hardly bother anyone at all. He is not in his right mind, and most people "over here" are disposed to turn a blind eye.

When he has one of his attacks, however, Yūichi's behavior takes on a much more positive character. Under the illusion that other people are troops under his command, he will shower orders indiscriminately on the villagers. By and large, a general distinction can be made: when he is not having an attack, Yūichi has the illusion that he is stationed at home, whereas during an attack he is stationed overseas.

During an attack, for example, he will quite suddenly bawl at a passerby, "You there—fetch me the NCO!" When the other hesitates, understandably at a loss in the absence of any NCO, he starts to bellow, "Well, look sharp there! What are you hanging about for, man?" At other times, he will unexpectedly issue commands such as "Charge!" or "Take cover!" Those recipients of his commands who are ordered to "charge" get off relatively lightly, since they can break into a run in strict compliance with his orders, thus making their escape without further ado. With the command to "take cover," however, the most one can hope for is to be in one's working clothes; if one is in one's best, it can be awkward. So long as the other man crouches down in the "cover" position, Yūichi is mollified, but if he hesitates to comply, Yūichi will shriek, "You goddam fool! You're under fire! Take cover!" and try his best to push him into the ditch. When this happens, the usual practice is for the other to take to his heels, whereupon Yūichi, being lame, has to give up the idea of chasing after him; nevertheless, the cries of "Run away and I'll slaughter you, you bastard!" by which the fleer is pursued are distinctly alarming.

However bad the attack, Yūichi normally steers clear of the very young and of the fair sex. His commands are directed strictly at the able-bodied men, and even then only at inhabitants of Sasa-yama district whom he knows by sight. The implied suggestion that Yūichi is rather particular about whom he chooses to carry out his more exacting demands prompted a rumor, at one stage, that his madness was feigned. At another time, a theory was current that his language showed he had no experience of army life at all. Nowadays, however, the theory generally accepted by the villagers is that Yūichi considers the able-bodied men of Sasa-yama, and no one else, to be troops under his command.

There are exceptions to this rule, however. On one occasion—long ago, during what was only Yūichi's second or third attack following the end of the war—two young men who had come to the village to buy vegetables for the black market were resting by the wayside shrine, when Yūichi happened to come past. "Target, three hundred!" he declared, much to their astonish-ment. "Goddam fools!" he chided them almost immediately. "What are you dithering for? You're under fire!" Utterly de-moralized, the two young men inquired no further, but fled in abject confusion. The war was only just over, and in all likelihood the vegetable brokers were intimidated by a certain authority they sensed in the military phraseology. This was a hangover, no doubt, from wartime days, when military language was something no one could afford to ignore.

Only recently, too, Yūichi issued an order to someone who was a stranger to the village. This was during what was perhaps his thirtieth or fortieth attack. A young man from a town on the coast came to the village to buy stocks of charcoal and was enjoy-ing a smoke at the wayside shrine with Munejirō, a villager who owns some forest land in the hills, when Yūichi sallied forth and issued the command "Take cover!" The young man was wearing a soldier's cap and army surplus uniform, which must have encouraged Yūichi in his delusion. Hearing the command, Munejirō prudently dived beneath the wooden veranda of the shrine on which they were sitting, but the young stranger remained seated. "Cover! You're under fire!" shouted Yūichi imperiously, and, gripping the young man's shoulder, tried to shove him beneath the veranda.

"What the hell? Why you—!" Thrown off balance, the young man shoved Yūichi's hand away.

"Defy me, would you?" cried Yūichi. "Idiot! Any objections and I'll slaughter you!" Yūichi promptly got a smart blow across the cheek.

"Defiance, eh?" He dealt the young man a slap in return, and the two began to fight in earnest. In trepidation, Munejirō crawled out from beneath the veranda, only to find Yūichi already knocked flat on his back and the young man in the old uniform undoing his belt with a view to giving Yūichi a good hiding with it.

"No you don't!" cried Munejirō, grabbing him round the middle. "Help—Hashimoto! Come here, will you? Hey—Shintaku! Come and give me a hand!"

Both Hashimoto and Shintaku lived on the other side of the road from the shrine. In swift response to the call for aid, they came running out of their respective houses.

Fortunately, the young man in the uniform was not well endowed with physical strength, and with Munejirō's arms encircling him from the rear, he threshed his arms and legs about in vain. Vocally, however, he displayed a considerable command of the fashionable vocabulary of the day.

"Listen to him—slaughter me, indeed! He's a relic of militarism, that's what he is! A bloody corpse! Here, Munejirō, let me go now! Come on, let me go, Munejirō! Surely you wouldn't deprive me of my freedom at such a critical moment?"

"Come on now, take it easy!" said Munejirō. "Look what you're up against—what can the likes of *him* do to you?"

"No! What does he mean, 'slaughter me'? That's the kind of

language that the relics of militarism use! It makes my blood boil just to hear it!"

"Come off it! Just think a moment—you'd put up with it all right if only it was wartime, wouldn't you? They used it all the time during the war. We're all in the same boat, aren't we?"

"What d'you mean, Munejirō Matsumura—what do you mean, telling me to act as if it was wartime? That's the kind of remark you just can't get away with. This is a country that has renounced all armaments. If you're going to talk like that, I'm going to return all the charcoal I bought from you!"

"All right, return it then! I don't fancy selling it to the likes of you anyway!"

Taking advantage of this altercation, Hashimoto and Shintaku had raised Yūichi to his feet. He seemed to have hurt his lame leg and managed to stand only by passing his arms round the shoulders of his two attendants. His face was white. His eyes were bloodshot and narrowed at the outer corners, so that his features resembled one of those fox masks that they sell at toy shops. The expression was past conveying any particular emotion, but most certainly Yūichi was burning with righteous indignation.

"Hey!" yelled Yūichi, gazing about him. "I want an NCO. An NCO! NCO—slaughter this man! He's a hindrance to operations. I want an NCO! Slaughter that man! It affects the men's morale under fire. Hey, aren't there any NCO's about?"

"Monster!" snarled the young man in the old uniform, as though loath to give up the battle. "Fascist relic!"

"Now see here, Yūichi," said Hashimoto, turning him, in his capacity as attendant, to face the other direction. "Let's go home, shall we? Right, Lieutenant! An outflanking movement in the face of the enemy!"

"Outflank the enemy!" bellowed Yūichi as his attendants led him away. "Operational order No. 22! One: the corps' main strength will deploy to face Kuala Lumpur city, while one detachment will make a detour into the hills to bring pressure to bear on the enemy's flank. . . ."

"Lot of bloody rubbish. Puffed-up bastard, fancying he's a soldier. Stupid pawn of aggression," fumed the young man in uniform. "Here, let go of me! Let go, will you? Come on now, Munejirō—I've got to give that half-witted leftover another piece of my mind before he goes."

But Munejirō was in no hurry to relax his restraining grip on the young man. Only when Yūichi had disappeared round the corner of the stone wall did he say, "That's all right, then. Sorry I had to do it," and removed his arms from around the other's middle. Now they could say whatever they liked about Yūichi.

At such times, Yūichi, on being escorted home, would be shut up in a cage in the outbuilding. The cage was boarded on three sides, with stout wooden bars on the fourth; the floor, too, was covered with sturdy boards. The attack was usually over within a couple of days; on the second or third day, his mother would go around apologizing to the neighbors, and only then would the door of the cage be opened. He could not be left shut up inside, since he was needed to work in the fields and to help his mother cover umbrellas, the work with which she supplemented their income. Without Yūichi's earnings, a family consisting of mother and son alone, with no other resources, would very soon find itself in dire straits.

The neighbors were well aware of this. It was the neighbors who, when Yūichi had been injured on active service and sent back to Japan with his brain affected, had gone to the army hospital to petition for his release. The neighborhood association had brushed aside his mother's protestations and had passed a resolution calling for Yūichi's release from the hospital; they felt that it was a proud thing for the association to welcome a homecoming officer into its midst. The authorities at the army hospital, having already satisfied themselves that Yūichi was of no further use to the military, allowed him to leave on a provisional diagnosis of palsy.

During the war, of course, there were adequate allowances, so that mother and son could keep going even without covering umbrellas in their spare time. Nor, at that stage, were Yūichi's attacks too noticeable. In the early morning, he would walk through the village streets in military uniform with a sword at his side, greeting in an encouraging kind of voice any able-bodied man in Sasayama whom he happened to encounter. Mostly, the salutation was something simple such as "Rise and shine!" though at times it was "Rise and shine. Come on now, no slacking!" Should he, as occasionally happened, encounter a party of people going to see off troops leaving for the front, he would command the party to make a halt and would deliver a simple but inspiring address. This was not a message for the benefit of troops going to the front, but an exhortation designed to foster the spirit of service and self-sacrifice in the seeing-off party, delivered on the assumption that they were troops under his own command. Even so, nobody at the time openly found anything comic in his behavior. His habit of walking early in the morning wearing military uniform was seen simply as exercise to improve the lame leg. It was only as Japan's defeat became imminent that people began to wonder at his way of carrying on. And it was not until several days after the end of the war that he showed unmistakable symptoms of mad fits.

At first, the villagers attributed these fits to some unpleasant malady contracted on service in the South Pacific. Before long, however, they began to conjecture that the disease was congenital syphilis—a theory which, perhaps because of its sensational attractions, gained considerable currency at one stage. Yūichi's father, who had married into his wife's family and property, had died in the same year that Yūichi had entered primary school, the cause of death being septicemia, a result of overwork and of malnutrition due to poverty. His mother, finding herself a widow, had sold the torreya tree at the back of the house in order to buy herself a set of summer clothes, and had gone to work as a live-in maid at an inn that stood near the station in the town on the coast.

Her earnings were surprisingly substantial. By the time Yūichi left middle school, his mother's work had put the family in a position, if not of affluence, at least of freedom from immediate worry.

The thatch on both the main building and the outbuilding was replaced by tiles. A hedge of Japanese cedars was planted around the grounds, and enormous concrete gateposts were set up at the entrance to the garden. The latter were added for good measure, without any relevance to the garden and the surrounding scene, but the neighbors nevertheless could hardly fail to be impressed by the will to succeed that had made his mother lay out so much money on such a detail.

Naturally enough, the family acquired a certain social standing. The gateposts, in fact, were admired in no uncertain terms by the village headman himself. He had dropped in at Yūichi's one day— he happened to be passing by, he said—and had delighted Yūichi's mother by singing the praises of her posts. A few days later, he had visited Yūichi's home along with the primary-school headmaster, and had declared in his mother's presence that he would recommend Yūichi as a suitable candidate for cadet training college. The reasons, he declared, were that Yūichi was a bright pupil, that Yūichi's mother was a woman of character, and that theirs was a model family. His mother was overcome with joy. After the headman and his companion had gone, she went to the Hashimotos and related the whole proceedings.

"Really, I can see now," she concluded, "that I did well to have those gateposts put up." She must have been rather overexcited, considering her usual composure.

By this time, the war on the continent had spread, and schools connected with the army were taking in vast numbers of pupils. Even those military schools that accommodated the lowest age-groups were falling over each other in their haste to acquire large numbers of boys, and the military authorities were resorting to a system of recruiting whereby schools in cities, towns, and villages throughout the country were directed to recommend children for the examination. Yūichi was one of those who were accepted. From cadet college, he went to officers' training college, and at the age of twenty-two received his commission as a second lieutenant. It was in December of his third year as platoon leader that he was sent to Malaya, and in January of the following year, at Kuala Lumpur in central Malaya, the order came promoting him, subject to confirmation, to first lieutenant.

Most of this the inhabitants of Sasayama were familiar with, having heard it from Yūichi's mother. Of what happened subsequently, they knew nothing. His mother was unable to give any account to the neighbors, since Yūichi himself said not a word. If his brain was affected so that he had lost his memory, then nothing could be done about it, but even inquiries as to his lameness elicited an almost completely blank expression and not even the vaguest of answers. Since this was somewhat reminiscent of the traditional reluctance of wounded soldiers to talk of their own experiences, Yūichi's taciturnity was at first attributed by the neighbors to a commendable self-effacement. After the end of the war, however, things changed to the point where he came to be cited by the neighbors as a good example of how the sins of parents are visited on their children.

At normal times, when he was not excited, Yūichi presented a placid exterior, and provided he did not catch sight of any able-bodied men with time to spare, might well have passed simply as the uncommunicative type. He could help in the fields and cover umbrellas. He was even sufficiently skilled to operate a rope-stranding machine. He might be only half there, but it was too much to believe that he had no idea at all of how he had become lame. People could hardly be blamed for thinking that there must be some correspondingly powerful reason why he should hesitate to speak of it. Even in the army, they reasoned, Yūichi's insistence, in his language and behavior, on service and self-sacrifice must have seemed overdone; it was quite possible that a colleague had complained to him about it, that they had fallen to blows, and that he had broken a leg as a result. Thus the theory evolved that he had broken his leg in a fight with someone with whom he had quarreled.

It was around the time when this theory had finally become generally accepted among the neighbors that Munejirō's younger brother, Yojū, was repatriated from Siberia. On the train south from Tsugaru, Yojū found himself next to a former sergeant-major called Gorō Ueda. Although he originally came from a village deep in the hills of Yamaguchi Prefecture, Ueda proved to be familiar with a folk song from Yojū's birthplace called "Home We Go." The song was one that children of Sasayama would amuse themselves by singing, pulling up new shoots of grass one at a time as they sang. The words, rustic and artless, were like those of a children's rhyme. It was good for singing, too, as one gathered reeds:

> Home we go, then, home we go,
> Empty baskets, home we go.
> Came to Hattabira pond,
> But the jay was crying there
> And the meadows were quite bare.
> There we gathered grasses but
> All the stems that we had cut
> Fell out through the wicker, so
> Empty baskets, home we go.

"Hattabira" was the name of the pond, a gourd-shaped pond that had been formed by damming up a stream in a hollow of the hills behind Sasayama. The children of the village would often go to cut grass in the meadow by the pond, which was only about five hundred yards round and lay in a grove reached by a woodcutter's track branching off from the road up the hill. It lay quiet, full of perfectly unremarkable, faintly cloudy water—the kind of insignificant pond that a stranger would never notice. Yojū, homeward bound from Siberia as he was, naturally felt a surge of nostalgia, even about such an uninspiring scene as that presented by the pond. Still more, though, he was startled and overjoyed that someone from another part of the country should know "Home We Go."

"Where did you learn that song, and who taught you?" he inquired curiously.

"I picked it up on a troop transport just before the Pacific War started," Ueda replied. "It's called the 'Sasayama Children's Song.' I'd say it comes from some really out-of-the-way place in the country, wouldn't you?"

Ueda had first learned what he called the 'Sasayama Children's Song' on his way to active service in the South Pacific. Whenever the soldiers gave an amateur show on board the transport, an officer in charge of a platoon, Yūichi Okazaki by name but popularly known as "Lieutenant Lookeast," would sing this song, so that the troops had picked it up in the natural course of events. It was no wonder, then, that Sergeant-major Ueda had given "Hattabira" its dialect pronunciation of "Hattabyura." The inhabitants not only of Sasayama but of the whole area pronounced it in that way. Starting with this talk of the pronunciation of "Hattabira," conversation between the two soon began to gain momentum. From Ueda, Yojū heard in detail how Yūichi had been badly hurt in Malaya, and he was able to inquire in detail into the circumstances that had made Yūichi queer in the head.

Former sergeant-major Ueda, who told him all this, had been a lance-corporal on the Malayan front in a platoon commanded by Yūichi Okazaki. He had, in fact, been Yūichi's own orderly. Yojū was the same age as Yūichi, but had been transferred to Mukden before Yūichi had gone to the front in Malaya, and knew nothing about Yūichi's mental state. . . .

Yūichi had been shaken off a truck, breaking the shinbone of his left leg, and had lost his wits at the same time.

They were on a journey by truck from Kuala Lumpur to a town called Selembang. The unit was approaching a small village called Seldang, when they came across troops of an engineering unit working on a bridge. In the river a concrete bridge lay destroyed by bombs, and members of the engineering unit were removing the massive lumps of concrete debris and building a humpbacked bridge of wood. The river was no more than five yards wide, but it is situations such as these that make soldiers in a truck unit feel most foolish. They can do nothing but wait, or at most help the laborers until the work on the bridge is completed.

The man in charge of the engineering squad was clad in an army cap and a loincloth. "You're unlucky, sir," said this half-naked fellow to Yūichi. "Twenty minutes earlier, and you'd have had a bridge. But then you're lucky, you know," he added. "Twenty minutes earlier, and likely as not the whole lot of you'd have gone up in smoke, trucks and all." Engineers, by and large, are poor talkers.

The work, they were told, should be completed within an hour or so. They had built a bridge that morning, but it had been destroyed by enemy bombing around noon, so they had built another, only to have it blown up again.

To avoid air raids, the whole unit, supply vehicles and troop trucks alike, were parked in a grove of rubber trees, and ten of the men went to help carry materials for the bridge. The rest of them waited with loaded guns in case there should be a raid. The reinforcement unit likewise took refuge in a rubber grove.

There had just been a shower, and it was cool among the rubber trees. The river, curving into sight through a gap in the rubber trees opposite, cut straight across the meadows and disappeared again behind a hillock. Here and there in the meadows were great holes where bombs had fallen. They had filled with rain to form small ponds, and in one of them two water buffaloes were soaking companionably in the muddy water, with only their heads above the surface. A white heron could be seen perched on the horns of one of the buffalo. Bird and beast alike were perfectly still, as though spellbound by the sight of the engineers at work on their bridge.

The work finished, the unit was crossing by truck when the leading truck came to a halt in the middle of the bridge and refused to budge. The engine had broken down. Repairs took time, and all the troops, those in the stalled truck as well as those waiting behind, took off their shirts. The trucks were cool when in motion, but, packed tight with troops as they were, the heat under the blazing sun was unbearable when they halted. Some of the men began to talk idly, in loud voices. The troops in the stalled trucks were particularly vociferous. Someone pointed at the buffaloes soaking in the craters in the meadow and wondered aloud how they would be to eat. Buffalo meat, volunteered another man, smelt strong and was tough and poor in flavor. Someone else, slowly counting aloud the number of craters, got as far as thirty-two.

"Extravagant, I call it," someone said. "Just look at them craters on that bit of meadow. They drop bombs like they'd got 'em to spare."

"An extravagant business, war is," said a lance-corporal called Tomomura. "Extravagant. War costs money, it does." Their voices were audible even to the orderly in the second truck, so they naturally reached the ears of Lieutenant Lookeast, who was seated by the driver of the same truck as Tomomura.

Lieutenant Lookeast got down from his seat. "You there, Lance-corporal Tomomura!" he said sharply.

A hush fell over the soldiers on the stalled truck. The lieutenant strode across the bridge to the halted truck.

"Here, let down the tailboard," he ordered. The troops on the truck opened up. He clambered into the truck and pulled up the board behind him.

"Lance-corporal Tomomura! Come here a moment, will you?"

"Right sir, coming!" responded Tomomura, and squeezed his way through the crush to the lieutenant's side.

"You—" the latter demanded, thrusting his face into Tomomura's. "What did you say just now? Let's hear it again, just as you said it then!"

"Sir, I said it was an extravagant business."

"Was that all? Repeat it to me in more detail, what you said just now."

"Sir, Lance-corporal Ōkaya said the enemy was dropping bombs as though they'd got them to spare. So I said that war was an extravagant business."

"Fool!" Whack, came his open palm across Tomomura's cheek. Again he hit him, and had just raised his hand to hit him a third time when the whole truckful of soldiers suddenly lurched. The driver had edged the truck forward slightly in order to test the engine.

His troops merely lurched, but the lieutenant, who was standing at the edge of the truck, did not get away so lightly. The tailboard, which was not fastened, fell open. Simultaneously, the lieutenant lost his footing and fell off the edge, grabbing at Tomomura as he went.

A startled exclamation arose from the soldiers. Clinging together, the lieutenant and Lance-corporal Tomomura toppled off the edge of the bridge, then bounced off the side planks into the river below. As luck would have it, the debris of the concrete bridge lay in wait for them below. The lieutenant fell face upwards onto the obstacle. Tomomura fell on his head and rolled off into the river. It was all over in a few seconds.

General uproar followed. The first to act was a warrant officer called Yokota, who dived into the river. "Quick!" he shouted. "Look for Lance-corporal Tomomura. One section of you, Sergeant Ōta in charge!"

Ueda, the orderly, was one of those who jumped into the river with the rest. The water only came up to the navel and the current was not fast, but their boots sank into the clay of the riverbed, hampering effective action. Before long, a medical orderly, who must have found a firm foothold somewhere, came swimming downstream.

"Sir! Sir!" Warrant Officer Ōta shouted pathetically in the lieutenant's ear. The latter lay on his back, eyes shut, with blood running from his ears. The medical orderly, who wore nothing but a loincloth, took the lieutenant's wrist and felt his pulse.

"I think he's all right. His heart's beating."

"All right? Really all right?" countered the warrant officer.

"Mm. . . . I think so," replied the orderly doubtfully.

By laying timbers from the bank across the concrete debris, one of the engineers made a passage across which a stretcher could be carried.

The troops who had gone downstream to look for Lance-corporal Tomomura were walking along the river stripped to their loincloths. It was difficult to see anything in the muddy waters of the river, so some of them were in the water, walking in zigzag fashion downstream. Tomomura had struck his skull on a lump of concrete, and might already have been unconscious when he fell into the water. If so, then according to the medical orderly he would not drown in the water; yet in the end they failed to find him. Fate had repaid him in ample measure for his innocent remark that war was extravagant. He had been struck across the face just before he died, and forced to join in another's tumble off a stalled truck. To add insult to injury, he had struck his head on a piece of concrete and been swallowed up by a muddy stream without even a proper name. A perfect miniature, one might say, of war; "extravagant," Tomomura might have complained, was hardly the word for it.

Restored to life, the lieutenant did nothing but heave painful sighs, so it was decided to carry him to the field hospital by stretcher rather than by truck. What seemed to them like sighs were doubtless, in fact, the faintest of groans.

By way of a grave for the soldier called Tomomura, they stuck a branch from a rubber tree in the ground by the river to mark his assumed last resting-place. It was because Ōkaya had remarked on the enemy's lavishness with bombs that Tomomura had exclaimed about the extravagance of war. Roughly ten percent of the re-sponsibility for Tomomura's bizarre fate rested, Ōkaya declared, with himself. Another twenty percent lay with the driver who had started the stalled truck without notice. As to who should shoulder the remaining seventy percent of the responsibility, he had no idea, he declared. But the implication was plain: the culprit was the platoon leader who had clung to him as he fell from the truck.

As they were all about to set off, the warrant officer ordered the whole unit to fall in. He drew his sword, and to the command

"A silent prayer for the soul of Lance-corporal Tomomura!"
they saluted in the direction of his hypothetical grave.

Tomomura had been, in every respect, a slow-moving fellow.
He himself had said that the general sluggishness of his responses
might well be divine retribution for the fact that he had always
been a timid child and had dodged innumerable sports meetings
while he was at school. He had a protruding lower lip and a long
chin, to disguise which he cultivated a goatee; the beard was
long, and he had the habit of stroking it in "at ease" periods
during roll call and the like. The lethargy of his movements was
counterbalanced by a remarkable skill in catching frantically
fleeing chickens. He could catch the fowls that ran at large in the
rubber groves with all the facility of a man going about gathering
up wastepaper baskets. Even when they fled, terrified, beneath
the raised floors of the Malayan houses, he could lure them
out again and into his hands with no trouble at all. This only
happened, however, when the aim was roast chicken for himself
and the other members of his squad; an awkward-minded man,
he was just as likely to chase the birds in all directions if he was
asked to do the same for another squad. On one occasion, an army
cook had gone to Tomomura and asked him to catch three or
four gamecocks, as they wanted to hold a cockfight. By chance,
it was the very day in Kuala Lumpur that Lieutenant Lookeast
had had informal notice of his promotion to first lieutenant, and
second lieutenants from two or three other platoons were with
him in his temporary quarters.

"So you'll have your cockfight," said Tomomura to the cook,
"and *then*, I suppose, the platoon leader will eat the cocks. The
officers are having a party to celebrate his promotion, if I'm not
mistaken. If that's so, you can count me out!"

In fact, it seems, the cocks were not for a party but for the army
cooks to have a cockfight with, but the story reached the lieutenant's ears nevertheless. The cook spoke to Warrant Officer Yokota,
and Yokota, rather than be disagreeable to the platoon's cham-
pion fowl-catcher, passed it on privately to the lieutenant.

The latter, however, was not a man to show his emotions over trifles. For all that his face revealed, he might never have heard a word of Warrant Officer Yokota's confidential report. Such tittle-tattle doubtless seemed inappropriate to him at a time when he had only just been promoted. Quite probably, in fact, his striking Lance-corporal Tomomura was totally unrelated to the episode of the fighting cocks, though how Tomomura himself and the soldiers round about interpreted it is another matter entirely.

As he was carried to the field hospital, the lieutenant lay face up on the stretcher deliriously repeating, "Here, let down the tailboard." Occasionally, he varied it with, "You, Tomomura, come here a moment, will you?" He said it not twice or three times, but over and over again, each time raising his hand painfully in an attempt to grasp the rubber-tree branch fastened over him to keep the sun off. Avidly his hand clutched at the empty air, as though seeking to take something in its grasp. The stretcher-bearer said it must be the effect of the fever, so Ueda moistened a towel with water from his flask and laid it on the lieutenant's forehead.

The field hospital was a Western-style private house standing with its back to a grove of coconut palms. A Malayan was trimming a flowering hedge, using a sickle with a three-foot handle. With his left hand on his hip, he wielded the sickle in leisurely fashion with his right hand, as though testing the feel of a tennis racket. Inside the iron-barred gate, which stood open, tall trees bearing fruit the color, shape, and size of snake gourds lined both sides of the drive leading to the entrance, creating a pleasantly cool shade. The lieutenant seemed to be defying the rows of trees as, clawing at the air with his fingers, he muttered incoherently, "Hey, let the tailboard down there. . . ."

Transferred from the stretcher to the examining table, Lieutenant Lookeast was found to be still wearing his open-neck shirt with military breeches and black boots.

"Why the devil didn't you take his boots off?" burst out the army doctor at Ueda.

"Well, sir, the left shinbone seems to broken. When we tried to take his boot off, you see sir, he complained of extreme pain."

"Well then, why the devil didn't you take his *right* boot off?" complained the doctor again. "The damned orderly's no good, that's the trouble." So Ueda removed the boot from the lieutenant's right foot, and handed it to a stretcher-bearer.

"There you are!" declared the doctor malevolently. "I told you it would come off, didn't I?"

As Ueda and the stretcher-bearer saw things, to let an army officer, and their own platoon leader into the bargain, wear only one boot was a reflection on their own dignity too.

"Cut it with shears," said the doctor to a square-faced underling in a surgical smock. "Cut the boot off!"

Questioned by the army doctor, Ueda gave his account of the situation at the time of the lieutenant's fall and the circumstances preceding his arrival in hospital. He also reported how blood had flowed from the lieutenant's ears, but he kept to himself the fact that the he had fallen off a stalled truck. A lance-corporal called Tomomura and the lieutenant had both, he reported, been shaken off when the truck ran over an obstacle and tipped to one side. "An act of God," he added gratuitously.

"What happened to this soldier call Tomomura?" asked the doctor.

"Sir, he was killed."

"The lieutenant wouldn't have been in the truck with his men," said the doctor. "He should have been in front with the driver. Out with it now—what happened?"

So Ueda told how Tomomura had spoken out of place and been struck by his commander. He also admitted that he had fallen as he was being struck.

Slit open vertically by the doctor's subordinate, Lieutenant Lookeast's boot soon lay on the floor. His military breeches were ripped open from the knee down. Thus exposed, the lieutenant's left leg was seen to be swollen—not merely the affected area, but the whole leg from the knee down. The doctor gave an injection of painkiller or some other medicine. "Hey there, Lance-corporal

Tomomura," muttered the lieutenant. "Just repeat what you said, will you?"

"I don't like the look of this at all," said the doctor with a portentous air. "Seems his brain is affected." He turned to Ueda. "He muttered something about Lance-corporal Tomomura, didn't he? I think the truck started off just as your commander struck the soldier. The truck was stationary, wasn't it?"

Hard pressed, Ueda admitted that this was so.

"Right then, you can go back to your unit. When you get back —no, it's all right. You just get back." By way of leave-taking, the stretcher-bearers and Ueda saluted their platoon leader lying prone on the examining table. As a result of the injection, he seemed to be drifting into a doze.

"He's a tough'un, that doctor," said one of the stretcher-bearers once they were outside the hospital entrance. "Picked on the weak points in the story and had the lies and the truth sorted out in no time."

"Of course," said his mate, "the old man himself had to come out with the wrong thing, too. No," he added hastily, "I don't mean the wrong thing."

"Look at that bastard there," he said, pointing at the man working on the hedge. "I envy these goddam Malays. It's not their own country, so they can leave wars to other people. Cutting the goddam hedge like he hadn't got a care in the world!"

"You'd better shut your trap!" warned the other, "or you'll find yourself in the stockade or worse."

Ueda lost his position as orderly and became an ordinary lance-corporal once more. A new platoon leader—a Lieutenant Asano, who had risen through the ranks—was assigned to the unit, and that same night two men were badly wounded in a night skirmish. The soldiers who carried them to the field hospital went to see how their former commander was progressing before they came back. His condition was not too promising. The leg injury, which included a vertical fracture, was definitely expected to heal, they were told. But the injury to his head had been aggravated into something internal. "What they mean," explained Mochi-zuki, one of the soldiers who had been to see him, "is that they started with a man with a bruise on the head, and suddenly he was plain nuts."

The lieutenant, Mochizuki reported, lay face up on the bed hardly speaking at all, and even then incoherently. Most of what he said, moreover, was restricted to military terms and the kind of words used in army pep talks. Even the excerpts from the pep talks, consisting as they did of fixed expressions, were very frag-mentary—threatening phrases on the lines of "Self-sacrifice and service," "Your lives in my hands," "Anti-military thinking," or "Any complaints and I'll slaughter you!" Since the terminology of the pep talks included a wide range of other specially devised phrases besides these, he suffered from no lack of choice.

"He's had it, though, if you ask me," said one soldier who went to the hospital. "Real simple-minded, he is. It's like he was full of drink."

"I can't say it too loud," said his mate, looking about him furtively, "but you know what I think? If you ask me, Lieutenant Lookeast's haunted by Tomomura's ghost!"

Ghost or no, the fact was that all the soldiers in the unit knew what had happened at that fateful instant. A definite percentage of the platoon's members had, with their own eyes, witnessed that moment when their commander, falling off the stalled truck, had grabbed hold of Lance-corporal Tomomura. The story was no fabrication of Ueda's.

The condition of the hospitalized Lieutenant Lookeast was made known thereafter by the reports of the stretcher-bearers who took new casualties from the platoon to the hospital. The fracture was guaranteed to mend. The dementia had likewise abated to a con-siderable degree, and he had reached a point where he did not, at least, talk deliriously. But the symptoms he had now, it was re-ported, were likely to continue indefinitely.

Around this time, a good half of the men in the unit had fallen prey to jungle sores. Most soldiers who had been through marshy terrain or fording rivers in the jungle areas caught the trouble. First, a skin infection similar to athlete's foot would break out here and there on the lower half of the body, then sores developed that gradually ate deeper, creating gaping holes. Countless of these holes, several millimeters in depth, would develop on the back of the legs, the shins, in the groin, and on the genitals. The medical orderlies did their best, with applications of mercuro-chrome, to get rid of this mysterious affliction, but for a while it raged virtually unchecked. Lieutenant Lookeast in the hospital, they said, had jungle sores all over the lower half of his body. Even after a night under canvas, any good piece of news about the war was enough to set him bowing towards the east, and he always preceded it by ablutions performed even in the dirty water of a ditch—which was how he contracted the disease. Nevertheless, a patient had only to move to an area where the water was pure for the trouble to clear up immediately.

Lieutenant Lookeast had always been fond of bowing to the east. Even on board the transport, he would have his men fall in on the deck, bow towards the east, and give three cheers whenever some good news came over the radio. Then he invariably gave a pep talk. Let the radio so much as report the bombing of a town on the continent by Japanese Army planes, and he would summon his men on deck to pay their respects towards the east. He would make them bow at the midday news, then have them bow once more in the evening for a repetition of the same news, so long as it reported a victory. As a result, the unit began to be called the "Lookeast unit" or the "Lookeast platoon," nicknames thought up for it by men in other platoons and companies.

This did not dismay Lieutenant Lookeast; in a pep talk one day after they had all bowed to the east, he declared that since the platoon had become celebrated for bowing thus, it must imbue its obeisances still more deeply with the spirit of self-sacrifice and service. "If only you read the Field Service Code deeply and thoughtfully enough," he added, "you too, my men, will, in a great flash of light, suddenly perceive the wonderful truth behind

43

our bowing to the east. Once you begin to understand it, it will fill you with a kind of intoxication."

Lieutenant Lookeast seemed even fonder of haranguing the troops on board the transport than of making his men bow to the east. One soldier suggested snidely that he only had them do it so that he could deliver his address afterwards. Another theory claimed that all the big talk was a bluff to cover up a fear of submarines. One soldier actually wondered aloud why the commanders of other units never told him to put a curb on his devotions. The other troops in his unit would have liked to ask the same question, but, as Lance-corporal Tomomura put it, "I expect you have to do more damn-fool things than that before you violate military regulations. It just shows you how easygoing the army is. But the likes of us have only got to have an undershirt pinched and it's a serious crime." Tomomura had been a man fond of speaking his own mind, to which extent he had, undoubtedly, been a poor soldier.

"I expect you'll be seeing Lieutenant Lookeast, won't you?" said former sergeant-major Ueda as Yojū started getting ready to leave the train. "If you do, tell him something, will you? Tell him that Ueda, his old orderly, told everything he knew about him. For his sake, he gave up more than two hours of scenery along the Sanyō line without so much as a glance. You'd hardly have thought he was a man seeing his native land for the first time in so many years. Just tell Lieutenant Lookeast that."

"That message is a bit of your Russian-style sarcasm, I suppose? If Yūichi gets the point, I'm sure he'll be furious! You forget he's supposed to be the incarnation of self-sacrifice and service."

"Like hell he is! I wouldn't mind betting he's been one of the first to change his tack. Either that, or he's still off his nut."

"I'd like you to see the concrete gateposts outside Yūichi's house. You'll never understand him properly until you've seen those. The posts have got bits of colored glass set in the top. Though *that* was his mother's idea, of course."

44

"Oh yes, and I expect there are some nice phrases from one of his pep talks carved on the back and front of the posts, aren't there? Anyway, you tell him when you see him—the soldier who was driving the truck at the time was severely punished. Albeit unwittingly, they said, he had injured an officer and sent a comrade-in-arms to an untimely death. That was the charge. And it was all thanks to my lord Lookeast's excesses. I tell you, it's one outrage after another in the army!"

Former sergeant-major Ueda hated Yūichi, he declared. At one time, he had felt only fear for him, but now the fear had been replaced by an irrepressible sense of loathing.

On the day that Yojū got back to Sasayama, Yūichi, alias Lieutenant Lookeast, had rushed out of the house under the influence of one of his attacks. Being lame, he is bad at walking, but he can get up steep slopes that put a strain on any normal person. When he comes down a slope, however, he walks slowly, where the ordinary person would have to rush. It seems that he has something in common with women who are possessed by the spirit of a fox, who, as is well known, will walk up a slope or a hilly road with no more effort than if it were flat ground. Even so, such women are incomparably more agile than Yūichi. If one goes to catch them on a hill over on the east, one only finds that they have given you the slip and are now standing on the hill on the other side of the valley. Their swiftness is the ultimate in the mysterious; they are bewilderingly elusive. Such transcendental flights are remote from Yūichi. Whenever his mother comes after him to catch him, he pretends to run away, then hides in a neighbor's outbuilding or creeps inside a chicken coop. Sometimes he dodges people by holing up in the night-soil shed. No, Yūichi is not so much supernatural as plain cunning. Remarkably enough, though, he never flees to other sections of the village, so he can be left to his own devices and little harm is done.

That day, Yūichi's mother, after an hour's fruitless search hither and thither, finally, shedding tears of self-pity, gave up the search for her son. Yūichi, in fact, was in the cemetery up on the hillside, walking up and down between the rows of gravestones. As he walked, he struck at each stone with his belt, lashing out with an enthusiasm that suggested that he saw the stones as his troops.

"Take that!" he muttered as he went. "And you, you swine . . . and you. . . . Take that! And you. . . ."

He was still at it when Yojū, who had arrived home that day, appeared with Munejirō, Hashimoto, and Shintaku, on a visit to the grave of his ancestors.

Munejirō carried lighted incense and a teapot. Yojū carried a spring of sasanqua with a half-opened bud. Hashimoto carried a dish bearing a large bun stuffed with bean jam. Brushing aside Yojū's insistence that he rejected all religion, they had brought him to report his safe return at the grave of his ancestors. According to Yojū, it was against his principles to visit an ancestral tomb, which was a relic of the feudal era and a symbol of religious conformism. Hashimoto let him have his say, then said soothingly, "Now don't say that, Yojū. When in Rome, you know. . . . If you don't behave, you'll find yourself without a girl to marry you. Anyway, I don't see anything to stop you visiting your ancestors' grave."

"You did as the Romans did when you were over there, Yojū," added Shintaku, "so I don't see why you can't do the same in your own village. There are all kinds of things in everyone's life that one has to turn a blind eye to. . . ." He changed the subject. "But it's good to see you back, though. We were all worried about you. Well then, let's go to the graveyard shall we?"

Thus did Yojū finally decide to go to pay his respects at the ancestral grave. Since nothing his elder brother Munejirō said had had any effect, Munejirō's wife had privately gone to ask Hashimoto and Shintaku to come and help persuade him.

When the party finally halted before the grave, Munejirō placed lighted sticks of incense upon the grave and poured water from the teapot into the vase. Yojū placed the sasanqua in the vase, stood facing the grave, pressed his palms together before his chest, and offered up a silent prayer. The others, too, joined their hands and without a word bowed before the grave. This pleasingly unso-phisticated rite was scarcely over, however, when a loud voice suddenly sounded right by their ears.

"Platoon! Fall—in!" came the command.

They turned to see Yūichi standing directly behind them in an army cap and a sleeveless jacket, glaring at the party. His eyes, narrowed at the corners, warned them that he was at the height of one of his attacks.

"Well, well, just as I thought—it's Lieutenant Okazaki," said Hashimoto with fine resource. "Nice of you to come, sir. We've got a special favorite of yours today." He took the bun off the grave where they had laid it, and pressed it into Yūichi's hand.

Yūichi glanced down at the bun and promptly raised it with both hands before his eyes in a gesture of gratitude. Such behavior was rare for him. What was more, though, his shoulders heaved and he began to snuffle. Finally, he transferred the bun into his left hand, and burst out crying in a voice like the howling of a dog.

The next moment he had stopped.

"Fall—in!" he bellowed hoarsely.

His eyes were narrowed again, and the sinews of his neck were quivering. Obviously, he was going to start ranting at them at any moment. At this stage, one must choose between two alternatives: to obey the command, or to grab Yūichi and take him back home.

"What do we do?" muttered Hashimoto. "Obey his order?"

"We don't want to spoil Yojū's visit to the grave," muttered Munejirō. "Shall we humor him just for today?"

"Come on, let's line up, then," said Hashimoto. "And Yojū," he warned, "mind you do as he orders!"

"Come along, now—quickly, men," said Yūichi, comparatively mildly. "Your equipment will do as it is. Quickly now, hurry!"

The four of them—Munejirō, Hashimoto, Yojū, and Shintaku —fell in with the tallest on the right and the shortest on the left.

"Atten—shun!" orderd Yūichi. "Right face! As you were!" He drew himself rigidly to attention and began to address them in solemn tones.

"You will pay careful attention," he began. "Today, His Imperial Majesty has been graciously pleased to send us a gift—of cakes. His Majesty has especially singled this unit out for his gift. There can be no greater honor. Nothing remains, I submit, but tears of gratitude. You will accept the gift with proper reverence. An official will now distribute them amongst you. First, though, we will face towards the east and bow in token of our allegiance. . . ."

At Yūichi's command, the four of them faced in the direction of Hattabira pond. The weather was cloudy, but they were aiming, quite accurately, eastwards.

The obeisance over, Yūichi stood them at ease and, advancing towards Munejirō at the right end of the line, gave the command:

"Attenshun! Open—*mouth*!"

The command was impressive, but the bun was a single one. Munejirō came to attention, turned his face upwards, and opened his mouth. Breaking off a small piece of the bun, Yūichi placed it in Munejirō's mouth. The next was Hashimoto. Yojū and Shintaku in turn also had a fragment of bun transferred into their mouths without mishap.

A good half of the bun still remained in Yūichi's hand. Coming to a modified attention, he turned his face upwards and stuffed the bun into his mouth. He was fond of sweet things. Forgetting to give the four of them the order to dismiss, he remained with bulging cheeks, not chewing, wishing apparently to savor to the full the flavor of the bun in his mouth. He was still doing so when his mother, unnoticed by him, came creeping up on him from the rear. It was to be expected that she would come to catch him, for his commands and the speech must have been plainly audible in their home at the foot of the hill.

All unawares, Yūichi stood with one palm politely covering his mouth, which was still full of the bun. His mother bowed slightly to the four worshipers, motioning with her eyes as though asking their help only if he should run away. The four assumed unconcerned expressions. Crouching down low, his mother moved briskly up to Yūichi and grabbed hold of the hem of his jacket.

"Yūichi, dear," she murmured in honeyed tones. "There's my Yūichi! So we're eating something nice, are we? Somebody must have given us something nice, then, mustn't they!"

Yūichi nodded with unexpected docility and opened his mouth to show his mother.

"Well, now! So they've given you a bun! Well, well, isn't that nice! That's our very special favorite, isn't it? So let's eat the bun as we go home, shall we? Come on dear, come home with me now. Please, dear. . . ." It was almost an entreaty.

Yūichi gave no sign of assent, but gradually things must have begun to penetrate, for he began to walk, hanging his head like one who is exhausted, as indeed he may have been. His mother, still clinging to the hem of his jacket, bowed briefly to the four men and set off beside Yūichi as he ambled homewards.

"What a relief!" exclaimed Yojū, spitting. "There's a God-awful relic for you!"

The other three spat too. Their spittle was dark and discolored with the bean jam from the bun. Yūichi had rolled the outside and the filling of the bun together into small balls to pop into their mouths, and none of them had had the courage to swallow the nasty stuff. Nor, coincidentally, had any of them felt like spitting it out before his gaze.

The four worshipers repaid their respects before the grave.

"Really, I feel sick!" said Hashimoto suddenly, spitting vigorously again. "He rolled the bun into balls with his grubby paws. But I must say, though, he's good at pep talks. Made you feel for a moment almost as though you'd really been sent cakes by the Emperor. The kind of speech that has the audience 'overcome with emotion,' as they say. What was it—'No greater honor than this. . . .'"

"Rubbish, the whole lot of it was!" said Yojū. "Nothing but a lot of playacting by madmen. A chorus by a bunch of men in jackboots."

"Easy does it, Yojū," said his elder brother soothingly. "Let's avoid aggravating each other, now. In my case, of course, I've nothing to do with it, so it doesn't really affect me. Even so, you shouldn't get worked up. The sight of Yūichi just now was what got you excited, wasn't it?"

"That relic from the past? Why, that dark spittle there's got more point for us than the likes of him!"

"Incidentally," said Hashimoto, "the daughter of the Ōmori's relatives in Inada village is a very nice girl, don't you think . . .?"

The other three waited expectantly for what was to come next, but he fell silent again. Taking their cue from him, they all walked down the hill in silence. It was a winding road that ran through a thinly wooded grove with its undergrowth well cut back. Through the trees, they could see down to the village street below, with a view onto Yūichi's house—tiled roof, cedar hedge, concrete gateposts and all. Usually, the colored glass that topped the posts glinted now red, now blue, but on a cloudy day it made a poor showing. They could see Yūichi and his mother trudging in through the gateway.

"And yet, you can't help admiring him," said Hashimoto, breaking the silence. "That Yūichi—he didn't make any mistake about which direction was east, did he? When you're in the cemetery, Hattabyura pond lies just due east, you know."

"Tomorrow's the day for draining Hattabyura pond, isn't it?" said Shintaku. "Yes, and the day after tomorrow its Botandani pond, I suppose. They come along fast one after the other at this time of year, don't they? Autumn's come early this year, so it'll be hard on the man whose turn it is to let the water out, the water being so cold."

"Right. And it's my turn this year, surely?" said Munejirō. "Here, Yojū—how about letting the water out for me? It's getting chilly, I tell you. And I've got a cold."

"That song about Hattabyura pond," said Yojū, ignoring the suggestion, "I hear it's getting quite famous these days. They say Yūichi was forever singing it on the transport going down south. Used to sing it every time the soldiers gave a show."

50

"All right, Yojū, I'll do it myself. So you heard about Yūichi singing in the south Pacific even though you were in Manchuria and Siberia? It must have been a sight, though, to see that stiff-necked martyr to duty singing a kid's song. Yes, I suppose the Hattabyura pond is famous these days. Isn't that nice? Yes, I suppose I'll have to drain such a famous pond."

Munejirō looked put out, realizing that his younger brother had skillfully diverted the conversation. He had put on an air of authority with the idea that his younger brother must not be allowed his own way in everything; he owed it to his dignity as elder brother.

As they came out into the village street and passed by Yūichi's house, his mother was drawing water at the well on the other side of the cedar hedge. The bucket had an iron chain instead of the usual rope. The well had been refurbished around the same time that Yūichi's mother had had the main house rebuilt and the concrete gateposts set up. The sound as the chain was wound up echoed shrilly around the whole village. It grated horribly on the ears, but even so the village headman had once praised the sound in the presence of Yūichi's mother. It was when he had brought the primary-school headmaster to suggest that Yūichi take the examination for cadet school. The headmaster, too, had spoken as though he were interested by the sound. There was a famous passage about the sound of an iron well-chain in the national reader they used at school; one of the finest pieces by a poet called Bokusui Wakayama, he had said.

"When you hear the sound from a distance," said the headman, waxing still more enthusiastic, "it's really just like the cry of a crane. What does the Chinese poem say? 'The crane cries deep in the marshes, its voice ascends to the heavens.' It signifies something very auspicious, you know."

The flattery was quite barefaced. Even so, for quite a time after that Yūichi's mother would draw more water than she really needed, so that the neighbors all about would hear the sound.

Pilgrims' Inn

I am staying here in Tosa on private business. For the most part, I am pleased to say, things have gone most satisfactorily. The only exception is that the day before yesterday I dozed off on the bus, and instead of getting off at a town called Aki was carried on to a place called Pilgrims' Cape. Thinking to make my way back to Aki, I was told that the last bus had already gone. It was fifteen miles to Aki, they said. So, my affairs being well in hand and with no need to get back quickly, I decided not to rush things but to put up for the night at Pilgrims' Cape.

The collection of dwellings at Pilgrims' Cape is officially known as Kimisaki, in the village of Pilgrims' Cape. There is no fear of losing one's way, for the village has only one street, lined on either side by low, single-story houses. Hoping if possible to find an inn with a telephone, I asked a passing fisherman, who told me that the only establishments with a telephone in the village were the post office and the police station. I inquired how many inns there were. Only one, he said: a pilgrims' inn.

True enough, at the entrance of the inn where I stayed, there hung a sign that said, "Pilgrims' Inn—The Waves." The inn as such has no pretensions of any kind, having a total of only three rooms for guests, but surprisingly enough there are three maids. On the other hand, there is neither proprietor, proprietress, nor proprietor's son. They are all employees, in fact, with no one officially in charge.

The first thing that occurred to me as I stood at the entrance of the inn was that it must be a fisherman's cottage, made over almost as it stood. It was already dark and I could not see the outside, but the papered sliding doors at the entrance and the low-hanging eaves were in no way different from those of the most ordinary fisherman's home. I opened the sliding doors and stepped into the narrow earthen-floored hallway.

"Good evening!" I called. "Is anybody there? I'd like a room for the night if you. . . ."

A sliding door opened from within, and a woman of around fifty appeared.

"Well, good evening to you!" she said. "A room for the night, is it?"

The door she had opened appeared to give straight onto the living room, and I could see a wrinkled old woman of around eighty and another woman of about sixty sitting by a charcoal brazier inside.

"Well, well, good evening to you!" they exclaimed as soon as they saw me. "Don't stand there, now," they added sociably. "Come right on through."

To get to the rooms at the back it was necessary to pass through the living room that led off the entrance hall. To complicate matters, the room was small, with small tables of food and a container of cooked rice set out for the evening meal, so that I could only get through by stepping over the charcoal brazier, a lacquered inkstone box, and sundry other objects. As I was stepping over the lacquered box, the oldest woman of all said, "Do come through, don't worry about us. But mind where you tread, please. The electric lamps don't give much light these days." And she rose with dignity to show me to my room.

The three guest rooms stood in a row, separated only by paper-covered sliding screens. The room leading off the one inside the entrance seemed to serve double duty as a guest room and a family room. A girl of about twelve and another girl of about fifteen were seated facing each other at a low table. They were dictating to each other from a school reader, but seeing me coming through they stopped talking and bowed. Both of them were rather bright-looking children. In the next room, a large man lay on his belly licking a pencil as he stared at an account book open before him.

"Excuse me," I said politely as I passed through the room.

"Uh? Oh, excuse *me*," he said absentmindedly. I was shown into the room beyond.

The very oldest woman got some pale blue quilts out of a closet. "These are for your bed, if you don't mind," she said. She left the room and was replaced by the woman of around sixty, who brought me some green tea.

"The toilet's just outside the sliding doors there," she said. "People have to come through here if they go in the night, so would you mind leaving the light on when you go to sleep? Will you be up early in the morning?"

I replied that I should probably be sleeping late.

"Well then, good night to you," she said. "Have nice dreams. How about dreaming," she added in an excess of affability, "of a shipload of treasure coming into port? That would be very nice, wouldn't it?"

I have never dreamed of a treasure ship in my life, nor do I ever want to. I spread out on the tatami the quilts that the oldest woman had got for me, took off my cloak and *haori*, and crawled in between the quilts as I was. A thin, hard quilt is often referred to as a "wafer quilt," but those that I now got into were like nothing so much as large dishcloths. I drew up my knees and turned to lie on my right side, facing away from the doors, so as to survey the room's amenities.

The wooden beams in the ceiling were completely exposed, and their blackened surfaces were stuck all over with pieces of paper of the kind that pilgrims making a tour of the shrines leave behind to mark their progress. One gave a name and an address in some country village. Another said simply, "May our great hopes be granted." I reflected on the fact that even people who stayed at squalid inns like this had their "great hopes" that they wanted fulfilled. Similar papers had even been pasted on a price list that was stuck on the wall. "Room per night, per person: thirty sen. Meals to order," read the list, which was written rather well in what seemed to be a man's hand. Someone who stayed there had probably done it for them. In one corner of the room stood a board for playing Japanese checkers, the usual massive block of wood but lacking its four small legs. Being the only piece of furniture in the whole room, its sole effect was to heighten the melancholy atmosphere.

I closed my eyes, still on my right side, having lost any interest in turning onto my left in order to study the pattern on the sliding screens. In the next room, I could hear the clicking of an abacus and the sound of small change being counted. Suddenly, there came the new sound of someone clapping his hands. The hands were clapped together at least ten or eleven times in succession.

"Yes?" came a voice in reply, from the room by the entrance.

"Bring me some saké!" shouted the man in the room next to mine, in a loud voice.

I draped a handkerchief over my face, and pulled the quilt over that in turn. I must have been very tired, for I felt I would go to sleep without trouble, and was still congratulating myself on the fact when I dozed off. I must have slept for some two or three hours. The next thing I knew, I had got my top half out of the quilts and had been awakened by a voice talking in the next room. It belonged, I felt sure, to the third woman, the one of around fifty, who was deep in conversation with my neighbor, keeping him company over his saké.

"No, not here," she was saying. "Though people often think so. The oldest of the three is Old Okane. The next is Old Ogin, and I'm called Old Okura. All three of us were abandoned here, you see. People who stayed at the inn left us behind. Foundlings, you could call us. . . ."

The woman seemed to be drunk; her voice, loud and clear, showed no concern for her surroundings.

"Yes, but surely one of the three is officially the proprietress?"

From the way he spoke, the man was drunk too. "Here, Gran," he went on, "have another. They say that saké's a wrinkle-smoother, you know."

The woman apparently accepted without demur the saké cup he held out to her. "Wrinkle-smoother—" she went on, "that's a neat way of putting it. I can't take much myself, but ten years ago Old Okane could get down a pint at a time. If somebody treated her to it, that is."

"Whose daughter is Old Okane, then? A pilgrim's, like the rest?"

"There's no way of telling," she said. "The old lady who was here before Old Okane, she too was left behind by someone who stayed here and she lived all her life here till she was old. The old lady before her as well, she started life in the same way. Besides, in this house we never let the babies know who their parents were. We've observed that rule from generation to generation. After all, there was no such thing as an inn register in the old days, was there? So no one knew the name of the foundling's real parents then, and even nowadays we never tell the children their family name or what their parents looked like."

"That means the girls who live here are foundlings too, I suppose? Now, I wonder what kind of people would abandon their children like that? For the life of me, I can't understand the mentality of such parents."

"Well, it was a good fifty years ago I was abandoned by my parents, so I've no way of knowing what they thought about it. I expect people are on their way to Pilgrims' Cape with a child on their hands and someone tells them about the custom at this inn. Generally speaking, I'd say there's been one baby left behind here every ten years or so."

"But isn't it funny that they're all girls?"

"Boys grow strong and get into trouble, so we chase after the parents and give them back. If we can't find where the parents have gone, we hand them in at the village office."

"How do you register them, then? Even with a girl, you have to register her at the office, don't you? She has to get married some day."

"Oh, no—we never get married. We consider ourselves as widows from the start; we stay on forever, in return for being brought up here. And whatever happens, we never get mixed up with any outsider."

"My, my . . . fancying holding out all those years!"

I draped my face with the handkerchief and pulled up the quilt so that I could sleep again. I found myself wondering at the oddity of the establishment. Even so, I doubted that the old woman had made it all up in a fit of drunken fancy.

The next morning, as I was leaving the inn, I compared the faces of the three women. The oldest of them was thin, with a narrow face. The second was short and fat; "barrel" would have described her quite accurately. The third woman was of medium build and height, and her features showed signs of having once been beautiful. The two children were nowhere to be seen.

"Have the children gone out, then?" I asked the youngest of the women.

"They're at school," she said. I grinned ruefully at myself for asking a stupid question.

Glancing at the doorway as I left, I saw two nameplates, fastened close side by side on the pillar. "Oshichi Kannō, Pupil, Pilgrims' Cape Village Elementary School," said one. "Okume Kannō, Pupil, Pilgrims' Cape Village Elementary School" said the other. The very oldest woman bowed to me politely as she saw me off at the entrance.

"Mind how you go, now," she said. "And goodbye."

On a stretch of sandy soil by the side of the inn, countless clumps of a thick-leaved evergreen plant were growing. I was much taken by the contrast between the dark gray of the sand and the green of their leaves.

Salamander

The salamander felt sad.

He had tried to leave the cave that was his home, but his head stuck in the entrance and prevented him from doing so. The cave that was now his eternal home had, as this will suggest, an extremely small entrance. It was gloomy, too. When he tried to force his way out, his head only succeeded in blocking the entrance like a cork, a fact which, though an undoubted testimony to the way his body had grown over a period of two years, was enough to plunge him into alarm and despondency.

"What a fool I've been!" he exclaimed.

He tried swimming about the inside of the cave as freely as it would allow him. When people are distressed, they frequently pace about their rooms in just this fashion. Unfortunately, the salamander's home was none too large for pacing about in. All he could manage, in fact, was to move his body somewhat to and fro and from side to side. This had the effect of covering the walls of the cave with slime and making them feel smooth, so that he was convinced in the end that moss had grown on his own back and tail and belly. He heaved a great sigh. Then he muttered, as though he had reached a great decision:

"All right—if I can't get out, then I have an idea of my own!"

But it scarcely needs saying that he had not a single idea of any use.

The ceiling of the cave was thickly overgrown with hair moss and liverwort. The scales of the liverwort wandered all over the rock, and the hair moss had dainty flowers on the ends of its very slender, scarlet carpophores. The dainty flowers formed dainty fruit which, in accordance with the law of propagation among cryptogams, shortly began to scatter pollen.

The salamander was not fond of looking at the hair moss and the liverwort. Indeed, he felt a positive distaste for them, for the pollen from the moss scattered steadily over the surface of the water in the cave, and he was convinced that the water of his home would eventually be polluted. What was worse, there was a clump of mold in each of the hollows in the rocks and the ceiling. How stupid the mold was in its habits! It was forever disappearing and growing again as though it lacked the will to continue propagating itself unequivocally. The salamander liked to put his face at the entrance and watch the scene outside the cave. To peer out at a bright place from inside somewhere dim—is this not a fascinating occupation? Never does one so constantly see so many different things as when peering from a small window.

Mountain streams, it seems, are given to rushing along in a great froth and flurry only to form large, still backwaters at unexpected places. From the entrance of his cave, the salamander could look out on just such a backwater of the stream. There, a clump of duckweed on the riverbed grew in cheerful array, stretching from the bottom to the surface in countless, slender, perfectly straight stalks. Then, when it reached the surface, it suddenly ceased its growth and poked duckweed blossom up from the water into the air. Large numbers of killifish seemed to enjoy swimming in and out between the stalks of the duckweed, for there was a shoal of them in the forest of stalks, all trying their hardest not to be carried away by the current. The whole shoal would veer to the right, then to the left. Whenever one of them veered to the left by mistake, the majority, of one accord, also veered to the left for fear of being left behind. Should one of them be forced by a stalk to veer to the right, all the other little fish without exception veered to the right in his wake. It was, therefore, extremely difficult for any one of them to make off by himself and leave.

Watching the little fish, the salamander could not help sneering at them.

"What a lot of excessively hidebound fellows," he thought.

The surface of the pool moved ceaselessly in a sluggish whirl-pool. One could tell this from a single white petal that had fallen into the water. On the surface, the white petal described a wide circle that gradually shrank in size. It increased its speed. In the end, it was describing an extremely small circle until, at the very center of the circle, the petal itself was swallowed up by the water.

"It almost made me giddy," muttered the salamander.

One evening, a tiny shrimp came wandering into the cave. The small creature, which seemed to be in the middle of its spawning season and had a transparent belly filled with what looked like tiny millet seeds, attached itself to the wall of the cave. For a while, it merely waved its tentacles, which were so long and fine that they disappeared before one could trace them to their end; then suddenly, for no apparent reason, it jumped off the wall, ventured on two or three successful somersaults in midair, and ended up clinging to the salamander's flank.

The salamander felt an urge to look round and see what the shrimp was doing there, but resisted it. If he moved his body even slightly, the small creature would certainly have fled in alarm.

What, he wondered, could this pregnant creature, this worthless scrap of life, be up to in this place?

The shrimp must be laying its eggs, under the impression that the salamander's flank was a rock. Or perhaps it was busy medi-tating on something.

"People who worry about things and get wrapped up in their own thoughts are stupid," remarked the salamander smugly.

He resolved that, whatever happened, he must get out of the cave. Nothing could be so foolish as to remain forever sunk in thought. This was no time for frivolity.

Summoning all his strength, the salamander made a rush at the entrance of the cave. But the only result was that his head stuck in the entrance hole, which it plugged tight like a cork. Thanks to this, he had to exert all his strength once more, tugging his body back in order to uncork it again.

All this commotion stirred up great clouds in the water of the cave, and the shrimp's dismay knew no bounds. At the same time, though, the sight of one end of what he had believed to be a club-shaped rock suddenly behaving like a cork and just as suddenly pulling itself out again made the shrimp laugh dreadfully. There is no creature quite like a shrimp for laughing in muddy water.

The salamander tried once more. Once more in vain. Invariably, his head got stuck in the hole.

Tears flowed from his eyes.

"Dear God, you are too unkind! It is tyrannical to shut me up for life in this cave just because I was heedless for a mere two years or so. I'm sure I shall go mad at any moment!"

In all probability, the reader has never seen an insane salamander, but it would be rash to deny all such tendencies in this one. The reader should not sneer at our salamander. He should appreciate that by now he had been immersed in his murky tub long enough to make him sick of it, and had reached a point where he could bear things no longer. Is not even the worst lunatic only longing for someone to release him from the chamber in which he is confined? Surely, even the most misanthropic of prisoners in jail desires just the same thing?

"Dear God, why was I, of all creatures, doomed to this miserable fate?"

Outside the cave, two water spiders, one large and one small, were playing on the surface of the pool, the smaller one riding on the larger one's back, when the sudden appearance of a frog alarmed them and sent them fleeing hither and thither in a series of hectic zigzags. The frog thrust up powerfully and rhythmically from the bottom towards the surface, showed his triangular snout briefly in the air, then thrust down again towards the bottom.

The salamander, who had been gazing at all this lively activity with considerable feeling, realized eventually that it might be better to avert his eyes from things that caused him emotion. He tried closing his eyes. It was sad. In his thoughts he likened himself, among other things, to a scrap of tin.

Nobody, I imagine, likes making absurd comparisons between himself and other things. Only to a man whose heart is wrung with grief would it occur to liken himself to a scrap of tin. How deep, indeed, he stays sunk in thought, with his hands thrust in his pockets! How he wipes his sweaty palms on the front of his waistcoat! No, there is no one like him for striking a whole variety of poses according to his particular fancy.

The salamander made no attempt to open its eyelids; for to open and shut his eyelids was the only freedom, the only possibility that he had been granted. What a mystifying thing took place behind his eyelids as a result! The simple formula of closing his eyes gave him command of a vast blackness. The blackness was a gulf that stretched away into infinity. Who could find words to describe the depth or breadth of that gulf?

I would implore the reader once more: do not, I beg, scorn the salamander for being so banal. Even a warder in a jail, unless he is in a particularly difficult mood, would scarcely reprimand a life prisoner for giving vent to a pointless sigh.

"Ah, the colder its gets the lonelier I feel."

No one with an attentive heart could have missed the salamander's sobbing from inside the cave.

But it is doubtful policy to leave anyone sunk indefinitely in sorrow. The salamander must have acquired a disagreeable disposition, for one day he stopped a frog who had strayed into the cave from getting out again. When the salamander's head corked up the window of the cave, the frog was so panic-stricken that he climbed up the rocky wall of the cave and leapt onto the ceiling, where he clung to the scales of the liverwort. It was the very same frog that had aroused the salamander's envy by shooting so vigorously from the depths to the surface of the pool, and from the surface back to the depths again. Should he be careless enough to slip and fall, the wicked salamander was there, waiting for him.

To place the other animal in the same situation as himself afforded the salamander exquisite pleasure.

"I'll shut him up here all his life!"

The curses of the wicked are effective, if only for a time. Stepping carefully, the frog got into a hollow in the wall. And believing himself safe, he put out his head from the hollow and said:

"I don't care!"

"Come out!" roared the salamander. And so started a fierce altercation between the two.

"I'll please myself whether I come out or not."

"All right. You can please yourself as long as you like."

"You're a fool."

"You're a fool."

Several times they repeated the exchange. The next day too, they maintained, in the same words, their own unyielding positions.

A year rolled by.

The warmth of the water in early summer changed the prisoners in the cave from lumps of mineral back into creatures of flesh and blood. So the two living creatures, accordingly, spent the whole summer in the following argument (it had already dawned on the salamander's companion that the salamander's head had grown too large to allow him to leave the cave):

"*You're* the one whose head gets stuck so you can't get out, aren't you?"

"No more can you get out of where *you* are!"

"Why don't you go out first then?"

"No—*you* come down from up there!"

Another year passed. Once more, the two lumps of mineral

were transformed into living creatures. But this summer they both stayed silent, each taking care lest his own sighs should be heard by the other.

In practice, it was not the salamander but his companion in the hollow in the rock who was first careless enough to heave a deep sigh. "Aaaah. . . ." went the sigh, like the faintest of breezes. It was the sight of the hair moss busily scattering its pollen, as it had done the year before, that had inspired it.

The salamander could hardly fail to hear. He looked upwards, and with eyes full of friendship inquired:

"You heaved a big sigh just now, didn't you?"

"And what if I did?" responded the other defensively.

"Don't reply like that. You can come down from there now."

"I'm too starved to move."

"You mean, you think you've had it?"

"I think I've had it."

It was some while before the salamander inquired again:

"What would you say you were thinking of now?"

"Even now," replied the other with the utmost diffidence, "I'm not really annoyed with you."

Old Ushitora

The Kasumigamori district of our village is divided into eastern and western sections by a winding road that passes through the village's very center. A river, also winding, tangles with the road as it runs down the valley. The people in the next village of Yaburodani, farther up the stream, must all pass along the main road through Kasumigamori whenever they visit any other village, for Yaburodani is surrounded on three sides by steep hills, the only side lying open being that facing Kasumigamori. Yaburodani, in short, is the village at the farthest end of the valley. When Kasumigamori children spot a child from Yaburodani passing through, they often cry out teasingly, "Old back of beyond!"

In Yaburodani, there lives an old man called Grandpa Ushitora. His real name is Torakichi, but since the first half of his name means "tiger," and since he is a past master of the art of rearing bulls, someone once dubbed him Ushitora, "Ox-tiger,"—two animals that stand adjacent in the Japanese zodiac—and the name stuck. His main occupation is providing bulls for breeding purposes. He also has a sharp eye, of course, for distinguishing between a good animal and a bad one. He can buy what seems an exceedingly ordinary calf and rear it into a fine, well-built bull. Cattle dealers from other parts often ask Grandpa the best way to rear cattle, but he invariably denies any special knowledge of such things.

A while ago, at a grand cattle show held jointly by two prefectures, Grandpa Ushitora's three bulls won awards. First, second, and third prizes all went to bulls entered by the old man. For the prizegiving ceremony, a representative came from the regional branch of a leading Osaka newspaper and took two photographs of the old man for publication, he said, in the regional edition. First he told Grandpa to smile and took a photo of him with his mouth open, thus revealing the gaps in his teeth; then he took another showing the old man stroking the head of the bull that had won first prize.

The same newspaperman also asked Grandpa some questions.

"I wonder, now," he said, "if you'd list your essential conditions for raising cattle? Of course, there's love for the animal, which I imagine is an indispensable item. And then, I suppose, one needs to be thoroughly versed in the habits of cattle. But isn't there some secret formula or other? This is a very important matter where stockbreeding is concerned, so I'd be grateful if you'd let us hear some of your ideas."

At a loss for a reply and with a large number of people looking on, Grandpa stood in some embarrassment.

"Now, Grandpa," spoke up an official from the stockbreeding section of the prefectural office, "surely there's some formula, some trick of the trade, isn't there?"

Grandpa thought for a long time and finally turned to the newspaperman.

"Trick of the trade—" he began, "now, I wouldn't know about that. One thing, though, is this: all the time, I treat my bulls as though I'd never kept a bull before. When I take them round with me, or cut grass for them, or put grass in their stalls, or clear away their dirty straw for them, or when I'm scraping them down with the brush, I take care of them as though I'd never done it before in my whole life."

All this the man from the newspaper branch took down on paper, nodding to himself all the while.

The newspaperman, who though young seemed to have an appetite for the unusual, went so far as to ask the old man the names of the three prizewinning animals. The winner of the first prize, having been bought at a place called Chiya, was known, it seemed, as "the Chiya bull." The winner of the second prize, which had been bought as a calf from a man called Heisaku who lived in Kasumigamori, was called "the bull bought at Heisaku's." The third prizewinner had been bought when still a calf at the monthly cattle market, and was known accordingly as "the bull bought at the market."

Such commonplace names were not, apparently, to the newspaperman's taste.

"Look here, Grandpa," he began in a discontented tone, "can't you find them some names with a more pastoral flavor? What we're really after is names with more local color—something with a more rustic touch, something that makes people long for their innocent childhood days. How would it be if you gave them some other names? 'Wild Cherry,' for example—that suggests the wild cherry blooming deep in the hills. Or 'Volga,' which suggests the boatman hauling his barge up the river, or 'Oak,' with its suggestion of fresh green leaves. Wouldn't you care to rename them, now, in honor of the occasion?"

The newspaperman was undoubtedly a kindhearted man or he would hardly, from the outset, have felt like writing an article about animals with such boorish names as "the bull bought at Heisaku's."

"Very well, then," said Grandpa, who saw no need to object, "I'll take advantage of that kind thought of yours. But I'd be much obliged if you'd just say those names again?"

"Wild Cherry . . . Volga . . . Oak." Grandpa repeated them to himself over and over again until they were firmly fixed in his mind. The winners of the first and second prizes were dubbed "Wild Cherry" and "Volga" respectively. The third prizewinner was named "Oak."

On his arrival back in Yaburodani, Grandpa notified his son of the change. His son, however, was highly embarrassed. The names, he declared, sounded like the names of coffee shops; just to hear them was enough to set his teeth on edge. The neighbors got wind of the disagreement but were obliged to admit, even so, that Grandpa's bulls had acquired a new dignity.

The newspaper reported the cattle show in the local news column of the regional edition, where it was dismissed in a meager three or four lines. All it said, in fact, was that Grandpa Ushitora's bulls had won prizes. Nevertheless, the same report brought a definite increase in the number of people who came to him to have their cows serviced. Hitherto, Grandpa had gone round the neighboring villages with his bulls, providing service at any house where a cow happened to be in heat. His bulls had always had a good reputation, and most farmers were already accustomed to rely on them to service their cows when necessary. Occasionally, a farmer would bring a cow specially to Grandpa's place, but since Grandpa's son objected strongly to the mating taking place at their home, Grandpa would go and call on the client later, taking the bull with him. His son, Tōkichi by name, was only a humble charcoal burner, but he could not agree, he declared, to his own father permitting such indelicate behavior; his whole being revolted against the idea. He even told the neighbors that if his father broke the taboo it would mean a severing of relations between parent and child.

Tōkichi had two children, a boy and a girl. Two years previously, when the boy had started at primary school, Tōkichi had made Grandpa stop taking his bulls about their own village. He felt sorry for the child, he said, because the other children at school looked at him oddly.

At first, Grandpa had told his son not to be so fussy.

"Now if you were a schoolteacher," he said, "I might listen to you. As it is, though, you're just a plain charcoal burner, so I'd be obliged if you'd be a bit less severe about what I do."

There is no family in the village that does not keep cattle, and some of the other schoolchildren themselves came from families that had their cows serviced as the occasion required. Why, Grandpa demanded, should those children take exception to his grand-son just because his grandfather took his bulls around? It was not as though a man who kept bulls for breeding was a kind of pimp; if anything, he was closer to a doctor. Tōkichi replied that it was because Grandpa took money for servicing the cows that the child felt so awkward. Anyway, he asked him to give it up for his child's sake; and Grandpa, for the sake of his beloved grandson, agreed to give up providing service at least in their own village.

In the event, getting Grandpa's name in the papers was, in a way, the source of all the trouble in Grandpa's family. Every week or ten days, an average of two people began to turn up at Grand-pa's place, bringing cows in heat. Grandpa pleaded an unwritten family rule as his excuse for refusing, but even so some clients would complain indignantly that he was hardhearted in turning them down when they had come such a long way. Some even made sarcastic remarks about people who put on airs. When his son was at home, Grandpa would send them away, saying he would call on them with the bull later. More often than not, how-ever, his son was away at the charcoal-burning kiln. Then, things were different; if a client came, Grandpa would choose a moment when his son's wife and his grandson were not looking to take the client and his cow into the woods, then take the bull to them a little later.

Even this ruse, though, was bound to be detected if repeated too often. One day, his son Tōkichi learned the truth from a charcoal buyer and came home in a towering rage. As soon as the evening meal was over and the two children were asleep, Tōkichi set about picking a quarrel with his wife.

"I simply don't understand," he declared. "I don't understand how he could give them such damn silly names in the first place. 'Volga'! 'Oak'! I told you, too, that you weren't ever to use such disgusting names. But you did, and now even the children do the same. It's enough to break up the whole family!"

At the sink in the kitchen, his wife, seeing storm clouds in the offing, went on washing the dishes in silence.

"A fine thing I heard today from the charcoal buyer!" he went on. "I never heard anything so shameful! But the truth always comes out in the end. He takes his bulls off into the woods on the quiet and mates them there for money. And you knew all the time, woman, but pretended you didn't! Mating cattle without telling people, it's immoral—it's adulterous, that's what it is!"

"I won't keep quiet any longer," Grandpa broke in, flinging to the ground half-made one of the straw sandals that he worked on at night to supplement their income. " 'Break up the whole family,' indeed! 'Adultery'! I don't know how you can talk such nonsense. What's adulterous about mating a couple of cows, I'd like to know? You'd probably tell a man he'd committed adultery if he saw a pair of dragonflies coupling in the woods."

"Whether it was in the woods or in the cowshed, I can't say," Tōkichi retorted. "I'm talking about something different. To mate them furtively and charge money for it, that's what's so degrading. If some outsider wants to bring his bulls to the cows, I couldn't care less. But not to know the distinction between the two things is awful. It's filthy! Ever since I was a kid I've had to suffer because of this same thing. That's why I became a charcoal burner. 'Oak'! 'Volga'! The very sound of them makes me want to throw up! I'm clearing out."

"What d'you mean, 'makes you want to throw up'?" demanded Grandpa. "Oak and Volga, I'll have you know, are a fine pair of bulls. And I'm an expert with cattle. My name was in the papers. If you don't like it here, you can get out. The more I put up with you, the more you take advantage of it. Clear out, then!"

Tōkichi, who was sitting cross-legged at the edge of the raised floor in the kitchen, shot to his feet and went off round the front. His wife chased after him but got no farther than the front entrance before turning back again. She knew perfectly well, either way, that Tōkichi's destination would only be the charcoal burners' hut.

Grandpa was beside himself with rage.

"He can please himself what he does! I'm going off round the neighboring villages with my bulls. I'm clearing out this instant. I've been patient enough. You, girl, you can tell Tōkichi that I've left this house for good. You can tell him that from me!"

True to his word, Grandpa set about making preparations for a tour of the villages.

This was the first time that Tōkichi's wife had witnessed such a serious quarrel between father and son. Minor differences of opinion there had often been, but the old man had always given in immediately and things had gone no further. This time it was different. Tōkichi had never used such harsh language to the old man before. Nor had the old man ever shouted at Tōkichi in such a loud voice. Tōkichi's wife was at a loss how to handle things.

"Grandpa, do try and calm yourself. Please!" she begged, making a clumsy attempt to bow with her forehead to the floor. "I'm apologizing for him, aren't I?"

"I don't want to hear it! I can take so much and no more. You tell Tōkichi that!"

Grandpa put on his long rubber boots. After that, he only had to fasten his wicker basket on his back and he was ready for the journey. Inside the basket there were two nosebags, blankets, sickles large and small, whetstones, a bamboo basket, brushes and a few other things.

The bulls were already bedded down for the night, but Grandpa led all three of them out of the cowshed. He would leave Oak, he decided, with Gosuke, a neighbor who was fond of cattle, and take the other two with him. Since the end of the last century, local regulations had forbidden lone cattle dealers to take more than two adult beasts about with them at a time. Besides, Oak was the youngest of the three; older bulls are liable to use their horns on human beings if beaten or struck—not, of course, that such a thing was likely at Gosuke's. The only animal Gosuke had was a calf, but he had four sons, so there would be no shortage of labor to look after Oak the bull. Children on country farms soon make friends with cattle, which also serve as playthings for them.

Gosuke was still up, busy at work making buckshot, with his

working gear scattered about the unfloored part of the house. He made the shot by melting lead and dropping it into cold water, each drop becoming a shot as it cooled. He was also a hunter, and would start making shot in his spare time before the summer was out, then sell it to other hunters and use the proceeds to buy his own cartridges.

"Gosuke, I don't like to ask you, but could you look after Oak for me? I'll go halves with you on the money I get for mating him if you like." Grandpa was still so excited that he offered to split the proceeds without even pausing to do his mental arithmetic first.

"What are you talking about, Grandpa? Oak? You're not serious!"

"Yes I am. Something's happened to me that I just can't stomach. Something very serious has happened to me."

Gosuke opened the door leading into the house. "Hey, stop that clatter!" he called to his wife, who was busily plying a hand mill in the kitchen. "How can we talk about important things with that row going on?"

Grandpa refrained from relating the bald facts and gave a rather romanticized version of the story instead. For personal reasons, he was setting out, this very instant, on a tour with his bulls. He would come back from time to time to fetch Oak for mating with a cow, but he refused ever to set foot in his own house. That was why he wanted Gosuke to look after Oak. This was definitely not a passing whim, nor was he doing it because he anticipated any failing in Oak's powers. He was rather weighed down at the moment, perhaps, by the uncertainty of existence.

Gosuke, who had been listening with a rather suspicious air, seemed to change his attitude at this and began to speak in serious tones.

"Ah, I see," he said. "I think I know that feeling. I have to kill living creatures myself, you know, when I go hunting. It must have been some fate that brought you here. . . . Right, leave him with me! He's my responsibility."

"He's in your hands, then. I've got him here outside the gate."

Following the custom among horse and cattle dealers, they clapped hands together three times to set the seal on the agreement.

Gosuke put Oak in the cowshed and chopped up some fodder for him. His wife held up a bicycle lamp for him so that he could see what he was doing. "Why don't we enter him in the cattle show next year?" she said gaily. "I wonder if there's a prize goes with it? You see, the name of the person entering him would be different, wouldn't it?"

"Shut your silly mouth, woman!" said Gosuke.

Grandpa Ushitora shone the flashlight round the cowshed. Oak was already lying on his side on the straw. The calf that had been there all the time was standing in a corner of the shed.

Gosuke and his wife saw Grandpa off up the slope back to the road. The old man was still angry about his son, but he managed to tell the story of his ginger and the moles, which had no bearing on his present situation at all. Twenty years previously, he had planted some ginger, but moles had eaten the whole lot. Gosuke responded by telling how, as a child, he had seen a stray dog running by with a mole in its mouth.

Back on the main road, Grandpa Ushitora set off walking, with Wild Cherry in front of him and Volga behind. The moon was not up yet but the sky was full of stars, and he began to feel rather easier in his mind. The clopping of the bulls' hooves and the sound of the stream running down the valley were not, after all, especially depressing. By the time a crooked moon rose above the hills, he had already reached Kasumigamori.

Grandpa let his bulls lead him to a house where they might call and not be unwelcome. Wild Cherry could always find, by some kind of sixth sense, a house where there was a cow in heat. Perhaps it was his sense of smell, or perhaps he heard the faintest of distant lowings that told him whether it was the right time for the cow and where she was. Or perhaps he just had a general idea of what was happening from frequent experience in the past.

"Off you go," said Grandpa. "Good hunting!" He flung the

rope up onto Wild Cherry's back and let the great animal lead the way.

Wild Cherry quickened his pace slightly and gave two great, mournful bellows. In response, the lowing of a cow came across the river from the general area of the wayside shrine in the eastern section of the village. It was the cow at Shuzō's place, just opposite the shrine. Wild Cherry had forgotten his reputation for finding a cow by his sixth sense and relied on her cries to lead him to her.

"Cunning beast!" grumbled Grandpa, with something like complacency, as he followed after him.

From time to time, Wild Cherry and Shuzō's cow on the other side of the river lowed to each other as though they had some secret understanding. Even Volga gave a bellow. Halfway along the narrow road from the main road to the eastern section of the village there was a narrow, earth-covered bridge. Beneath it, by the side of a still pool, stood a great shell-shaped rock. By night, without a moon, the bridge would have been dangerous, but Wild Cherry crossed it without the slightest hesitation and pressed ahead until finally he stopped in front of the cowshed at Shuzō's.

The cow in the cowshed was setting up a great commotion, snorting heavily and jabbing upwards at the crosspieces on the door with its horns in an attempt to open the door from the inside. Every year, she went into heat in an alarming fashion, but the previous year she had been serviced twice without producing any calves. That year too she had already been serviced once without result. She might well be a barren cow. Barren or no, her spells in heat were something terrible and set her rampaging about in great excitement.

Grandpa took his two bulls round by the outbuilding and tethered them separately to persimmon trees.

"Who is it?" demanded Shuzō, hastening out of the entrance to see what the commotion was about. In the light of the moon, he soon made out Grandpa Ushitora and his bulls.

"Well, Grandpa Ushitora!" he exclaimed. "Doing your round of the villages? You came at just the right time. My cow's been lowing all the time, and terribly restless. I came out to the cowshed any number of times to see what was up with her. There didn't seem to be anything I could do. But then you turned up. Talk about a fairy godmother!"

"I don't like to turn up late at night like this, without letting you know. . . ."

"Eh? Late at night? Don't be silly. Just look at that cow of mine. Look how restless she is, poor thing! And it's embarrassing with the neighbors, too, the way she gets excited when she's in heat."

Shuzō turned out the light he held in his hand.

Grandpa tied the cow in the shed on a short tether so that she could not jump about, then drove Wild Cherry into the shed. The mating was all over in a flash. To make sure that things took properly, Grandpa rubbed the cow's back for her. Then he drove Wild Cherry and Volga into the stable, which stood empty, and left them feeding on some sweet-potato runners that Shuzō had put in the manger for them.

Shuzō was in his forties and lived alone. He had no children. If he wanted so much as a cup of tea, he had to struggle to light the fire for himself beneath the kettle, filling the whole kitchen with smoke in the process. His wife had died the year before. Nothing could be done about that, Shuzō said; what really hurt was that people recently had begun to gossip about the cow. She was a typical barren female with sex on the brain, they said. The year before, he had had her serviced twice by Ushitora's bulls to no avail, so this year he had taken her to a place called the O.K. Breeders, a good twelve miles away. That did not take either. To make matters worse, every time she was in heat she bellowed and threw herself about as though she were half crazy, and had twice broken down the door of the cowshed during the night and run away.

The first time, the course she had taken was clear in every detail the next morning. She had fled to the rock garden at the Tsuruyas' nearby, where she had relieved herself on a rock covered with green moss. From there, she had gone on to the house of a widow who had a bull, and had stamped up and down in front of the cowshed. The widow's eldest son, drawn outside by the noise, had attempted to capture the offending animal, only to see it make off, swifter than any horse, in the direction of the Ashishina district of the village.

The next morning, Shuzō discovered the door of his cowshed smashed and the cow gone. Uproar ensued. Before long, news came from the Tsuruyas. A cow unknown had disgraced itself on a rock in their garden and made a clean sweep of the strips of giant radish hung out to dry over the veranda. Unless she was caught as soon as possible and given a dose of bicarbonate of soda, the dried radish would swell up in her stomach and choke her to death when she ruminated.

Pale at the thought of the terrible loss that threatened, Shuzō set off in search of the cow on his bicycle. Fortunately, he soon found her, tethered to a persimmon tree in one of the terraced fields on a hillside at Ashishina. She was only a cow, it was true, but to have created such a public disturbance, especially over a display of carnal lust, was disgraceful.

The second time she had run away had been on the twenty-first day following her servicing at the O.K. Breeders. On that occasion, she had run a full twelve miles in the middle of the night and gone back to the O.K. Breeders. As soon as Shuzō found in the morning that his cow had gone, he guessed where she was and went to the O.K. Breeders on his bicycle to fetch her back. Even a cow, he had reasoned, must cherish a rather special feeling for the partner made familiar from experience. Fortunately enough, his shot in the dark had hit the mark. Any delay, and the cow would almost certainly have been made off with by someone else.

She was a troublesome cow, indeed. Even so, Shuzō was fond of her and was determined, he said, to see her blessed with children. To have a calf would, he was convinced, put an end to her carnal preoccupations. Even while he was drinking tea in the kitchen, Shuzō got up two or three times to go and peer into the cowshed.

"Will it take or won't it?" said Shuzō anxiously. "I wonder. . . .

If it doesn't take this time, do you think it means she's barren?"

Such a question was not for Grandpa to answer; it was the province of the vet, after a proper examination.

They went to bed, their quilts laid out side by side on the floor, but Shuzō got up yet again to go and look in the cowshed. The cow was lying on her belly with her legs folded beneath her, peacefully dribbling as she ruminated. Even after he was back in bed, Shuzō started talking to Grandpa again. If a mating was not successful, it was natural for anybody's cow to go into heat again and there was no need for Shuzō to worry so much. If it wasn't successful this time, he said, he was afraid the cow would get excited and start rampaging and bellowing almost immediately. It humiliated him in the eyes of the neighbors. They would get the idea that her owner was the same way. He would willingly provide a bull for her just to keep her quiet; in fact, if that was the only purpose, any seedy animal from the nearest place at hand would do. And yet, for a man of his age and living alone to provide such a service was hardly respectable.

Grandpa himself had once been asked by a circus to provide just that kind of service. Twenty years previously, a cattle market had been established in Kasumigamori, and one of the committee members had invited a circus to the village for the opening ceremonies. The circus was made up of a dozen or so men and women who brought with them two horses, one cow, and a dog, and its performances consisted of putting the animals through various acts to make the audience laugh. Grandpa had been summoned to bring a bull to the circus.

The booths for the performances, simple affairs of frames covered with straw matting, had been set up on the dry riverbed in Kasumigamori. Arriving there with his bull, Grandpa was met by a large man in dark glasses, who looked like the manager of the circus and who asked him to do something about his cow, which was in heat. It didn't matter whether she got pregnant or not, he said, so long as she cooled off. To fill such an order was hardly going to increase the reputation of a cattle breeder. Then, to top it all, the man who seemed to be the manager asked him outright to see, if possible, that the bull didn't make her pregnant. "Damn fool," thought Grandpa, and went straight home again with his bull.

Unfortunately, the wrong story had got about. The tale that spread around was that old Ushitora, the cattle breeder, had put his bull to the circus cow to get her off heat rather than with calf: a bovine brothel, said people snidely. In a day or two, everyone had heard the story, not only in Kasumigamori but in Yaburodani and all the other villages round about. The net result was that Grandpa became a laughing stock, while the circus cow enjoyed an enormous vogue. The general impression seemed to be that she was in some way a seductive, flirty type of cow. Thanks to this, the circus had a considerable attendance, but on Grandpa's side his son Tōkichi, who was still at primary school, was ostracized by the other children for quite a while afterwards. On more than a few occasions, Tōkichi came home from school crying. Tōkichi had never forgotten how he had suffered at that time; that was why, even now, he was still oversensitive where breeding was concerned.

"Really, it's a nasty business," concluded Grandpa Ushitora.

"You could go on fretting about it forever. Let's go to sleep," said Shuzō.

The next morning, Grandpa woke up early. It was a fine day. Before breakfast, he went to the water mill to buy rice bran. On the way back, he dropped in at a shop where they processed bean curd and bought some of the sediment left after making the curd. Everything was intended as fodder for the bulls, but he set a little of the sediment aside and had Shuzō mix it with the rice for their breakfast.

Grandpa had just finished breakfast when he had a visitor. It was Uchida from Kasumigamori, who had found out somehow where he was. Then, almost immediately afterwards, he had another visitor. This time it was the former priest of the Myōkendō shrine in the western section of the village. Both of them, by strange coincidence, brought presents of sweet potatoes for the bulls, and asked him to bring his bulls for mating with their cows.

When Grandpa led the two bulls out of the stable, both Uchida and Myōkendō, as he was still known, asked to have the servicing done by Wild Cherry. Wild Cherry, however, was not for use for some time to come. Even with a bull in the prime of life, it is normal to mate him with no more than seventy to seventy-five cows in a year. Grandpa had always made it a rule to put Wild Cherry to work five times a month, and to get the other two bulls to help out with the rest.

The Myōkendō priest was much taken with Wild Cherry. "When all's said and done, you can't beat a Chiya bull," he said. "This one's the best of the bunch. A good, substantial animal!"

His companion Uchida also praised Wild Cherry to the point where Grandpa began to get embarrassed. His praises sounded so much like flattery designed for the ears of Wild Cherry himself that Shuzō interrupted him.

"Praise him as much as you like, the animal couldn't care less," he said. "If you praise him too much it sounds barefaced, like some marriage go-between talking."

"Well! So my cow's not the only one that gives trouble," said Myōkendō, making a sly reference to the unconventional behavior of Shuzō's own cow.

Grandpa received his payment from Shuzō, and got back onto the main road with his two bulls. Uchida and Myōkendō followed in their wake, vying with each other all the while in praising the way that Wild Cherry walked, the gloss of his coat, and so on. His appearance was, indeed, so fine that even the non-expert would have noticed it. He was massive and handsomely built, whether seen from the front or the side. His dewlap hung in ample folds from his chin and down his chest, as though the surplus weight of his body were overflowing into it. Viewed from the rear, his gait had a ponderous assurance. His thighs were pleasingly plump, his hips square-set, and his coat gleamed a dazzling black as he walked. His horns rose straight and even, glossy black at the tips and matt black at the base, as though they had been dipped in water.

Uchida and Myōkendō were each trying to let the other take precedence in having his cows serviced. There were another five days before Wild Cherry would be fit to use.

"No, after you," said Uchida. "My cow's only two years old. Whoever heard of a youngster taking precedence over someone older from the same village? My cow must certainly take second place because of her age, quite apart from anything else."

"No, no. *You* first. My cow's so shy, you wouldn't believe it. Last year, now, we had the bull brought twice, but she behaved as though nothing was up at all. This time too, I expect it'll take time."

After much give-and-take, it was finally agreed that Uchida's cow should be serviced first. Myōkendō's cow might or might not be bashful, but the fact was that Grandpa had taken his bull there twice the previous year, only to find that he had met his match. Myōkendō's cow had not given Wild Cherry—then still known as "the Chiya bull"—so much as a second glance. Slowly, as though she had all the time in the world, she had put herself out of his reach, though she bellowed all the while as though she was off her head, with bloodshot eyes and every other physical sign of being in heat. Having given birth to twin calves two years previously, she ought not to have objected to the mating, but for some reason or other she rejected his advances on both occasions.

Myōkendō, watching the proceedings, had grown desperate. "Come on," he had scolded her, "get some life into you! None of your airs and graces!" The second time, too, he had scolded her in the same way, afraid that the fee he paid was going to be wasted. Possibly the timing had been wrong on both occasions; most cows go into heat between twenty-one and twenty-eight days after parturition and are in heat every third or fourth week thereafter, but the period is a bare one and a half days, and even then, the first half day is the best.

Once the servicing of Uchida's cow was over, Grandpa went to cut grass on the embankment of the pond below the temple, then took Wild Cherry alone down to the river in the valley. He made him walk about in the shallows and washed him all over with a brush, then wiped the drops off him with a towel. He even cleaned the dirt off his hooves. Then he took the bull's hooves one at a time on his knee, and was scraping the underside with a sickle to improve their appearance when a voice hailed him:

"Well, Grandpa Ushitora! Haven't seen you for a long time! Cleaning his hooves, I see. A cow's hooves are surprisingly soft, aren't they?"

It was the younger brother of the previous head of the Tsuruya family. He carried a fishing rod, with a fisherman's creel in his hand, and his trousers were soaked through up to the knees. He was already in his early fifties, and the sideburns below his white hat were flecked with gray. Some thirty years ago, he had gone to Tokyo to study but had dropped out of school and, disqualified thereby from obtaining a job with a decent firm or government office, was said to have been making a living writing novels. For nearly two years during the war, he had brought his large family to stay with the Tsuruyas in order to escape the air raids. Even then, he had gone fishing in the river every day throughout the summer. When one of the neighbors greeted him with a "Hello! Going fishing?" he would reply "Off to work!" thus doing his own reputation a good deal of harm. This time—again, it seemed, with the purpose of tiding over a financially thin time—he had brought his son, who was on vacation. One could hardly expect much, at any rate, of a man who abandoned his birthplace and went off to knock around in foreign parts. To say that a bull's hard hooves were surprisingly soft was hardly a compliment. . . .

"It all depends on how you use the sickle," said Grandpa, giving him little encouragement, and went on paring.

"They say cows like being scratched here, don't they?" went on the Tsuruyas' visitor, pinching at Wild Cherry's dewlap. "In the Kantō area they call this part the 'hangskin,' you know. What would the cattle dealers in these parts call it?"

"We call it the 'hanging.' The '*throat* hanging.' "

"Is that so? The 'hanging,' eh? And how do you tell a cow's age? I hear there are all kinds of complicated ways of telling it, by the proportion of deciduous teeth to permanent teeth, or the extent to which the permanent teeth have been eroded. . . ."

"We here, we just look to see how many teeth it's cut, if it's a young animal. With an older animal, we look to see how much it's worn down its second teeth."

As soon as Grandpa had finished paring the bull's hooves, the Tsuruyas' visitor went down under the bridge and started fishing. Soon Grandpa appeared up on the bridge leading his bull, whereupon he hailed him again from below.

"Grandpa—perhaps I shouldn't bring this up now, but they do say you've left home. Somebody tipped me off about it a while back. But you know, Grandpa, traveling about never got anybody anywhere!"

He might almost have been talking about himself.

That night, Grandpa got Uchida to put him up. The next day, he took his bulls down to the broad, dry riverbed about two and a half miles downstream and turned them loose there. At night, he stayed at the general store near the bus stop; the owner was a distant relative. The store had a two-story outbuilding at the back, with a window looking out over the riverbed, which was convenient for keeping an eye on the bulls. The next day, and the following one, he slept on the second floor of the outbuilding; and all the while, as he watched over the animals, he tried hard to keep thoughts of his son's wilfulness out of his head, so that the bulls too could take their ease and relax.

On the fifth day, he set out early in the morning with his two bulls and went to the Myōkendō shrine in Kasumigamori. The cow there still showed no change, but the next morning she was definitely in heat. Contrary to Myōkendō's prediction made the other day, the cow proved neither bashful nor retiring. If anything, she was rather forward. When Wild Cherry came lumbering into the cowshed, she simply stood there motionless, as though stuffed.

That night, Grandpa put up with Myōkendō. With the latter's approval, he drove the two bulls into the outbuilding, which was all but empty, and gave them their nosebags with sweet potatoes in them. He opened the two windows high up in the walls as wide as possible.

Myōkendō's place stood on a piece of high ground, an offshoot of the hills. It had originally been a shrine dedicated to the Bodhisattva Myōken, but, since the war, serving the gods and Buddhas was no longer a profitable sideline, so the place had ceased to be a temple, and Myōkendō had returned to secular life as a farmer pure and simple. The hall that had housed the statue, the priest's living quarters, the cowsheds, and the outbuildings all stood side by side in a line, with a rocky cliff behind them. The remaining three sides formed a steep slope of red clay sparsely dotted with pine trees, with a narrow path winding up the slope. The site was quite well protected, in fact, but some intuition warned Grandpa that he should fasten the door of the outbuilding with nails.

Myōkendō laid out quilts for Grandpa in the very center of what had been the shrine and hung a mosquito net over it for him. He also opened up all the shutters, so that there was a pleasant breeze.

Grandpa was already in bed when Myōkendō came to worship before the statue of Myōken that still stood in the sanctuary at the back of the hall. Grandpa was just dozing off but woke up again.

"Well, well, Myōkendō," he said. "Time for prayers, eh? You mustn't mind if I go to sleep."

"Go ahead, go ahead. You know, it doesn't really pay to do this nowadays, but even so I say the sutras every ten days."

He lit a small candle in the candlestick standing on the altar. Then, rubbing his prayer beads between his palms, he said:

"Sorry to bother you, then. Afraid the sutras will disturb your sleep rather, but I'll start the service if you don't mind." And he started chanting the sacred scripture. It was quite impossible for Grandpa to go to sleep, but to get out of bed seemed rather too pointed, so he lay still and did nothing.

The sutra-reading over, Myōkendō apologized to Grandpa again.

"Sorry to bother you again, but I'll give the drum a bang while I'm about it, if you don't mind. I expect you can hear this drum way over in Yaburodani, can't you?"

"Yes, we can hear it at night over in my place."

"You know, it just doesn't feel right unless I give this a bang. Just to let people know we have the faith, you see. . . ."

He started beating the drum. He beat it with a fine abandon, and at the same time began chanting in a loud voice. It occurred to Grandpa, though he disapproved of his own thoughts, that if Myōkendō went at it like that, there must surely be the occasional person who came with offerings in a sudden fit of generosity. He could not help having this idea, so unpleasantly jarring was the sound. The noise must have stopped without his realizing it, however, for he soon fell asleep.

The next morning, disaster struck. Immediately on rising, Grandpa went straight to the outbuilding, where he found the door open and both bulls gone.

"Oh, my God!" cried Grandpa, stamping his foot, and set off at a run for the former priest's living quarters. Shouting he knew not what at the top of his voice, he pounded on the door. The commotion roused Myōkendō, who was still in bed. As soon as he heard the grave news, he started bawling at his wife, too, to get up. She came out wearing nothing but a nether garment, only to be yelled at angrily by Myōkendō. "Idiot! Loose woman! Go and get some clothes on!"

Marks on the outbuilding door suggested that the nails holding it fast had been pulled out with pliers or some similar instrument. In the unfloored downstairs section, only a single pile of cow dung was to be seen, and quite a few of the sweet potatoes were still left in the nosebags. Someone had apparently led them away the previous night, against their will, before they had got far into their potatoes.

"As I see things, this is what happened," said Grandpa. "The thief must have come during the night. It must be someone who knows this place well. That's how I see things."

"Right, right," said Myōkendō. "They almost certainly came while I was banging the drum. Must know how the land lies, eh?"

The former priest and Grandpa followed the tracks left by the bulls in the soil. Here and there on the surface of the red clay, hoofprints were visible.

"There were two of them!"

Myōkendō and Grandpa followed the tracks to the back of the shed. On the narrow road leading down from the garden, there were confused imprints of cattle hooves. At the very bottom of the road, there were footprints of rubber-soled socks and military boots, left in the sand that had been washed down by the rain.

"Three of them must have worked together. Perhaps as many as four. Odd way to go about things," said Myōkendō peevishly.

The hoofprints disappeared after crossing the earth-covered bridge over the river in the valley. An embankment covered with green grass led along the river from the end of the bridge. The culprits seemed to have taken the bulls along it, but the grass grew too thickly for footprints to be distinguishable.

"We have to report it at the police station at any rate, so I'll go downstream," said Myōkendō. "You go and look upstream."

"I don't think the thieves will have got very far. If a cow in heat bellows, Wild Cherry bellows back, doesn't he? So keep your ears open for any cow that calls."

Grandpa was just setting off along the path by the river when Myōkendō added: "And don't forget—it's important to ask around for any information likely to be useful."

The green grass that covered the path was wet with morning dew. From time to time, he noticed that the grass had been trodden down, but it seemed unlikely that cattle had passed that way. He hurried along the track straight along by the river. Eventually, it gave onto the main road. The question was whether or not there were any signs of cattle having passed that point.

The sun had not yet risen. The raised path along the river had been constructed to prevent flooding. The righthand side, over-looking the river, was faced with stones, while on the left a row of plum trees stretched for a good three or four hundred yards. The path led onto the main road at the point where the trees ended. Here, there was another earth-covered bridge, and at one end of the bridge stood a water mill, now deserted and tumbledown. Grandpa went back and forth across the bridge, hoping to find any tracks left by the bulls on the road, but found nothing that looked at all likely. He even opened the wooden door of the water mill. Once there had been an incident in which a young man from another village stole a cow from our village, slaughtered it secretly in the water mill, and discarded the bones at the back of the building.

Grandpa went inside and struck a match. The earthen floor was empty save for three millstones, on one of which lay a bunch of withered plum branches, left there, probably, by children at play. He looked out at the back and found a man there, fishing.

"Well, good morning!" said the other, looking up at Grandpa. It was the Tsuruyas' visitor again.

"Good morning," said Grandpa politely.

"You're an early riser, Grandpa. I was here fishing before it got light this morning. Caught quite a lot. Nice river you've got here in this valley."

"Glad you like it. . . . By the way, have you seen anybody go by with some bulls?"

But just then, someone came across the bridge on a bicycle, calling to Grandpa as he came. It was Uchida, who was wearing a cotton night kimono that stopped at his knees, plus high rubber boots.

"I just got the alarm from Myōkendō," he said. "Dreadful shock. No idea, he says, where the bulls have gone. We split up and rushed off in different directions to look for them. If we get wind of the criminal, the signal is two strokes on the fire bell."

"No sign of the bulls going along the main road, I suppose?"

"Nothing," said Uchida. "Nor where the path on the downstream side leads into the main road. Not so much as a chicken feather, let alone a hoofprint."

If the thief had made his escape along the main road with the bulls, he could only have taken them by truck, but there were no truck marks on the road either. The thief, Uchida said, might have fled into the hills. But the hills surrounding Kasumigamori slope up steeply from the back of the village, and it would be hard going to take refuge in them with cattle on one's hands. Even the road upstream came to a dead halt at Yaburodani.

"If they fled into the hills, they must still be lying low there. I wish a cow in a stall somewhere would give a call for a bull."

Cupping his hands, Grandpa imitated the sound of a bull lowing. The Tsuruyas' visitor gave up his fishing and produced a similar imitation. He gave his imitation with great gusto, in a much louder voice than Grandpa, then said:

"No reply. . . . You know, Grandpa, you really shouldn't have left home. Just supposing, now—only supposing, of course—that it was your own son Tōkichi who'd stolen the bulls. It would make a nice ending to the story, wouldn't it? If Tōkichi were back home with the bulls now, it would mean an end to your wanderings, wouldn't it, Grandpa? Or perhaps I'm a bit indiscreet to go making such predictions. Not that it's anything more than my wishful thinking, of course. . . ."

Grandpa could not have cared less whether it was indiscreet or not. Without even replying he made off at once, leaving Uchida to follow after him, pushing his bicycle as he came.

Carp

For more than a dozen years past, I have been troubled by a carp. The carp was given to me in my student days by a friend, Nampachi Aoki (deceased some years ago), as a mark of his unbounding good will. He told me that he had caught it far away, in a pond in the country near his home.

The carp at the time was one foot long and pure white in color.

I was hanging handkerchiefs to dry on the railing outside the window of my boardinghouse, when Aoki arrived with an aluminum bucket containing a large, white carp covered with a mass of waterweed, and made me a present of it. As a sign of gratitude for his good will, I swore that I would never kill the white carp. Enthusiastically, I fetched a ruler and measured its length, and discussed with him where I should keep it.

In the back garden of the boardinghouse there was a gourd-shaped pond. Its surface was littered with bits and pieces from the trees and bamboo, and I hesitated to release the carp in it, but after a little thought decided that there was no alternative. The carp disappeared into the depths of the pond and did not show itself for several weeks.

That winter, I moved to private lodgings. I wanted to take the carp with me, but having no net gave up the idea. Accordingly, once the equinox was past, I returned to the boardinghouse to fish for the carp. On the first day, I hooked two small roach, which I showed to the master of the house. He had no particular interest in fishing, it seemed, but was surprised that there should have been roach in the gourd-shaped pond, and the next day took his place beside me fishing.

At last, on the eighth day, I hooked the carp I wanted, using a silkworm grub. The carp was still as white as ever, and no thinner. But there were transparent parasites lodged on the tips of its fins. Carefully I removed them, then filled a metal basin with cold water and put the carp in it. I covered it with a fig leaf.

My lodgings, of course, had no pond. I thought, therefore, of killing the carp to have done with it, and many times I took the fig leaf in my fingers and tentatively lifted it. Each time, the carp was opening and closing its mouth, breathing easily and peacefully.

I took the basin to Aoki's to confer with him about it.

"I believe your girl has a large pond in her garden, doesn't she? I wonder if she'd take care of the carp?"

Without hesitation, Aoki led me to a place at the edge of the pond that was overhung by a loquat tree. Before releasing the carp in the pond, I stressed that although I was putting the carp in a pond that belonged to his mistress the fish itself was still unquestionably mine. Aoki gave me a look of displeasure; he seemed to take what I said as motivated by a mere desire to please. I had pledged to him earlier that I would always treasure the fish.

The carp sank deep into the pool, together with the water from my basin.

In the summer, six years later, Nampachi Aoki died.

Although I had often visited him on his sickbed, I had had no idea that the illness was serious. In my ignorance, I felt irritated with him when he would not even accompany me on my walks; and I smoked cigarettes by his bed.

I decided I would buy a cactus in the Formosan Pavilion at the exhibition held that year, and take it to Aoki as a present. But he died on the day that I arrived at his home carrying the pot. I stood at the entrance and rang again and again until his mother appeared, but when she saw me she started sobbing uncontrollably, and I could get nothing out of her. Then I saw all the shoes inside the hall, and among them the dainty, feminine shoes that Aoki's mistress always wore, so I placed the potted cactus on a ledge and went home.

At the funeral two or three days later, the potted cactus that I had given him stood on my friend's coffin, alongside the square, brown student's cap he had always worn. I felt a strong urge to get the white carp from the pond at his girl's place and take it home. The only time he had ever shown displeasure with me had been over the carp.

I made up my mind to write a letter to Aoki's girl. (I reproduce it here in full, lest Aoki's spirit should misinterpret my motives.)

Dear Madam,

May I offer my heartfelt condolences on the passing of Mr. Nampachi Aoki? I am writing to request your kindness in returning a carp (white, and originally one foot long) belonging to myself that Mr. Aoki, on my behalf, entrusted to your care in the pond of your garden. In this connection, I should be grateful if next Sunday, whatever the weather, you would allow me to use my fishing rod there, and if you would leave your back gate open from early morning on that day.

Yours respectfully. . . .

A reply came. (I have set down the full text here, lest Aoki's spirit should misinterpret his girl's motives.)

Dear Sir,

Thank you for your letter. I find it perhaps a trifle insensitive that you should ask to fish so soon after a funeral, but since you seem to attach extraordinary value to the fish in question, I agree to your request. You will excuse me if I do not meet you or even come out to greet you, but please do not hesitate to do your fishing.

Yours in haste. . . .

Early on Sunday morning, I crept into the residence of the late Nampachi Aoki's mistress, carrying a luncheon box, together with my rod, bait, and bowl. I was considerably agitated. I should have brought the reply to my letter with me, just in case someone found me.

The fruit of the loquat tree had already ripened to a golden yellow that inspired a lively appetite. I realized, moreover, that the plants and shrubs by the side of the pond were covered with such a fine display of foliage that they concealed me from both the upstairs window and from the platform on the roof. With the wrong end of my fishing rod, I knocked down one of the loquats. In fact, since it was getting near dusk when I finally caught the carp, I ended up by helping myself to a considerable number of the fruit.

I released the carp in the pool of Waseda University.

Summer came, and the students began to swim in the pool. Every day, in the afternoon, I would go to watch and to marvel, as I peered through the wire netting that surrounded the pool, at the skill with which they swam. I was out of work by now and the role of spectator suited me particularly well.

As sunset approached, the students would come out of the water and, without dressing, would sprawl beneath the lacquer trees or smoke and chat with each other. Many a deep sigh I heaved as I gazed at their healthy limbs and the cheerful sight they made as they swam.

When the students had ceased diving into the water, the surface of the pool seemed still quieter than before. Soon, several swallows came flying to the pool, where they fluttered and skimmed the surface. But my white carp stayed deep below the water and refused to show itself. For all I knew, it might be lying dead at the bottom.

One warm, oppressive night I lay awake till dawn. Then, thinking to get some fresh early morning air, I went and walked near the pool. At times like this, we are all prone to dwell on our own solitude, or to tell ourselves that we should find some work, or simply to stand for long periods with our hands tucked in our pockets.

And then I saw it.

There it was, my white carp, swimming about in fine fettle near the surface of the pond. Stepping quietly, I went inside the wire netting and got onto the diving board so that I could see every detail.

My carp, making the most of the space at his command, swam about like a king. And in his wake, anxious not to be left behind, swarmed many roach and dozens of dace and killifish, lending the carp that was mine a still more lordly air.

With tears of emotion in my eyes at the splendid sight, I got down from the diving board, taking care to make no noise.

The cold season came, and the surface of the pool was strewn with fallen leaves. Finally it froze. For that reason, I had already given up any idea of looking for the carp, yet still I did not neglect to come to the pool every morning, just in case. And I amused myself by throwing countless small stones onto the flat surface of the ice. When I tossed them lightly, they skidded swiftly, with a cold sound, over the ice. When I flung them straight down, they stuck into the icy surface.

One morning, the ice was covered with a thin layer of snow. I went and picked up a long bamboo pole, and with it drew a picture on the face of the ice. It was a picture of a fish and it must have been close to twenty feet long. In my mind, it was my white carp.

When the picture was completed, I thought of writing something by the fish's mouth, but gave up the idea and added instead a large number of roach and killifish swarming after the carp in fear of being left behind. Yet how stupid and insignificant the roach and killifish looked! Some of them lacked fins; others, even, had neither mouth nor eyes. I was utterly content.

Life at Mr. Tange's

Mr. Tange chastised his manservant. (Mr. Tange is sixty-seven, and his manservant fifty-seven.) The decrepit old man was forever taking naps in the middle of the day, and it was necessary, so Mr. Tange said, to have him turn over a new leaf. I have never seen Mr. Tange so angry before.

Peering out round the corner of the bathhouse, I watched the progress of the punishment. Mr. Tange brought three straw mats from the shed and spread them on the ground beneath the persimmon tree.

"Lie down on these mats!" he commanded the manservant.

The servant clung tightly to the trunk of the persimmon, foaming slightly at the mouth from nervousness. A chastisement, even in a remote rural spot like this, is taken very seriously. Mr. Tange pulled out the tobacco pouch tucked in the manservant's sash, and placed it on the mat. Then he said in a grave voice:

"You will lie down here on your back and smoke your pipe while we watch. That's what you always do, isn't it—you put your left heel up on the knot of the persimmon tree, and you lie back, and you rest your right heel on the shin of your left leg, and you go on smoking quite happily until it begins to get dark. So now we're going to stand here and watch you grandly smoking your pipe. Do you dare refuse to get down there quickly when I tell you?"

The manservant, pressing one arm against the place where the tobacco pouch had been tucked in his sash and clinging to the trunk of the persimmon tree with the other, made no immediate move to obey the order. Yet he had no idea of defying his cruel master.

"I never thought," he said, his cheek as he spoke almost brushing against the leaves of a plant of the orchid family that grew on the tree, "that I'd be told off like this just for sleeping in the daytime. I'll lie on the mat all right, but I have a feeling that if I do, something still more dreadful is going to happen to me."

"That's enough of your villainous talk! I'll let you off before long."

So the manservant took off his straw sandals and lay down hesitantly on the mat. Then he turned over and settled on his back.

"Strip to the waist!" shouted Mr. Tange.

Helped by Mr. Tange, the manservant pulled his kimono off his shoulders. His body was deep-chested and sturdy, but the rapid way his ribs rose and fell showed the strain he was under. It was apprehension, I am sure, as to the course his punishment would take. If he had had any idea of rebellion, or any desire to escape, his ribs would have heaved more slowly and massively.

Mr. Tange walked once round the mat and stopped by the head of the recumbent man. Then he commanded in a stern voice:

"Put your left heel up on the knot of the persimmon tree."

The manservant put his left heel up on the knot of the persimmon tree.

"Now why don't you rest your right foot on the shin of your left leg?"

The reclining figure did as it was ordered.

"Now light your pipe!"

Mr. Tange picked up the tobacco pouch from beside the reclining man's head, stuffed tobacco in the bowl of the slender pipe, lit it, and stuck it in the manservant's mouth. Smoke came out of the manservant's nostrils and ears.

"It's funny—" he gasped painfully, with the pipe still in his mouth, "you let me lie here and smoke my pipe, but somehow it doesn't seem like your usual kind self. And somehow it makes me feel still more guilty."

"Then why don't you be quiet and have a nap?" said Mr. Tange angrily, so the man on the ground shut his eyes.

"I can't go to sleep even if I try," he said to Mr. Tange without opening his eyes. "I'm sure it doesn't really look as though I'm having a nap, does it?"

"Why don't you go to sleep properly instead of talking when I told you not to?"

"You make it sound as if it was my fault."

Just once, the ribs of the man on the ground gave a great heave, then set to rising and falling rapidly as before. It must have been a sigh of hopelessness.

When Mr. Tange next spoke to the manservant, he had recovered a certain amount of his composure. It was wrong for a mere manservant, he said, to plant a gourd seedling by the well without his master's permission. He was also gravely at fault in having trained the branches of the pines in the garden without being asked, so that they looked even worse than before. The carp in the pond, too, had grown timid lately and fled to the bottom of the pond whenever they heard a footstep, which was obviously because somebody had teased them while the master was out. Mr. Tange said various other things as well but ended up saying:

"Look at you sprawled out there, as though you owned the place! Very comfortable for having a nap in the daytime, I'm sure."

"Don't be silly," said the man on the ground desperately. "I'm too worried."

Mr. Tange straightened his hat, took out his pocket watch, put it to his ear, shook it, and looked at the time. It must have occurred to him that he would be late for work. In great haste, he went out through the side gate. (Mr. Tange, I should note, is a hardworking government official. The nameplate on his gate says: "Ryō-tarō Tange, Revenue Officer, Joint Village Office, Himetani, Shigawa, and Imobara Villages."

Even after Mr. Tange had gone, the man on the ground was in no hurry to change his position. But I could tell that he was not asleep, for the pipe had not yet fallen from his mouth.

I told myself that I would reconnoiter for this unfortunate old servant to see how far Mr. Tange had gone. If Mr. Tange should merely have pretended to leave by the side gate, if he should still be dallying outside, it would only invite fresh disaster for the man lying on the mat to change his position. As he went to work, Mr. Tange always stopped to gaze around at the terraced fields and crops, and to pull up any weeds he might find in the stone embankment. Sometimes, he would grasp the ears of wheat in the terraced fields with both hands to reassure himself that the crop in his fields was better than anybody else's.

Gazing over the wall and down into the valley, I observed Mr. Tange walking down the main road with urgent steps. He wore his hat pushed back on his head, and went both uphill and down at exactly the same pace. It takes a man born and bred in a country valley to maintain such an even pace on slopes.

I attracted the attention of the old servant still lying on the mat.

"I think it's safe to get up now. The Revenue Officer is just going. I don't expect he'll be back until dusk."

At this, my companion opened his eyes, the pipe fell from his lips, and he raised his head from the mat to gaze about him. Then, seeing me looking down at the valley from the wall, he got up, rubbing his hip as he did so.

He came over to where I was standing at the wall, but kept himself hidden behind me so that his employer, even should he look back as he walked down the road in the distance, would think it was only I who was peering over the wall. In fact, Mr. Tange did look back from time to time as he went down the road, but the chance of his noticing the true state of affairs was negligible.

At short intervals along both sides of the road there were clusters of trees, and I could spy Mr. Tange in the gaps between them.

"There's nothing more to worry about," the manservant concluded as, shielded by my body, he slipped his bare arms back through his kimono sleeves. "If he goes off to work at the village office swinging his arms out from his body like that, it means he's not angry with me any more. I've watched him go from here ever since I was so small that I could hardly see over this wall. I used to bring a stool and stand on it on tiptoe, and do you know, as I watched him go I'd pray that he'd come back soon. To think that for dozens of years I've watched him leave here without missing even once. So you see, however I'm chastised, I must never take his words lightly, just as it's important that I always see him off. That's so, don't you think?"

On the road in the distance, another man was coming from the opposite direction, walking towards the Revenue Officer. The Revenue Officer and the man came together just at the point where the road touches the stream running down the valley. An enormous rock lies in the stream just there, and the waters of the stream were sending up white spray as they dashed against it. Mr. Tange took off his hat and the other removed the towel tied round his head in order to exchange greetings, which they did by bowing with their hands on their knees, bending at the knees at each bow.

"That's Yōnoji," muttered the manservant at my side.

The man called Yōnoji began smoking. The Revenue Officer began, too. They embarked on a lengthy conversation, waving their arms and bending from the waist as they talked.

"Yōnoji," explained the manservant as we watched him in the distance, "arranges the sales of timber from the pinewoods and the mixed woods. He seems to be getting quite worked up, doesn't he? You can tell at a glance even from here."

Yōnoji the broker, the manservant said, knew the names of all the forest owners in the district as well as the average ages of their trees. He was always going to the timber merchants in the big towns and supplying them with various bits of information; he knew, for instance, when the pines on Mount Noro in Imobara were just right for cutting into one-foot planks, or that the owner of a certain wood had to hold a service to mark the seventh anniversary of his father's death, due on the fifteenth of next month, and would be only too glad to sell the pines on his land to defray the expenses. In return for his services in arranging a deal, he received one-hundredth of the price from both the timber dealer and the seller.

"It looks as though Yōnoji's just getting down to arranging the deal, doesn't it? I'm sure he's trying to arrange a sale for the pinewood at Takitsuse in Shigawa."

The two small figures on the distant road had begun bargaining over the price, using the method of putting their hands alternately up each other's sleeves. Putting his hand up the other's sleeve, Mr. Tange bent backwards from the waist. Doubtless he was laughing. Next, the broker too put his hand inside Mr. Tange's sleeve and bent backwards, then he wiped his forehead with his towel. The two of them went through the same motions any number of times, until finally they drew themselves up rather more formally and began to clap hands in time with each other.

"Clap, clap, clap. . . . Clap, clap, clap. . . . Clap, clap, clap," went their hands in rhythmical groups of three. We did not hear the last three until the figures in the distant scene had finished clapping. The road ran straight and unbroken along the bottom of the deep valley.

The two distant figures adopted the same positions as a while ago, with their hands stretching down to their knees, then set off walking in opposite directions.

For certain, we told each other, a contract for the sale of some pinewood had been concluded. With his nail, the manservant drew a rough-and-ready map for me in the plaster of the wall. It was a map of the pinewood at Takitsuse in Shigawa village. Here, where the ground dipped, the trees grew thickly, and it would take the lumberjacks a good four hours at least to fell a single tree. He'd a mind, the manservant said, to go straight to the pinewood to see whether the trees there grew thickly or not. But then, perhaps he'd better not; they said that trees deep in the woods would not grow if they were looked on too often by human eyes.

The next day but one, a letter came for the manservant. He showed it to me and asked me to read it for him. Mr. Tange seemed envious that his employee should have received a letter. "This time, *you've* got a letter," he said, "but at the New Year, I got as many as sixteen New Year's cards." And he made no move to read the letter for him.

The letter was inscribed "Private and Confidential." The manservant, I found, was called Eisuke Tanishita. Mr. Tange always called out "Ei, Ei!" when he wanted to summon his manservant. The name of the sender was Otatsu Tanishita. I opened the envelope.

"Is it all right to read it?" I said. "It says 'Private and Confidential.' " The writing on the envelope had obviously been written for the sender by somebody else.

The manservant took me out beneath the persimmon tree and had me read it aloud for him. The whole letter was written in a childish script and an abominable style.

"Just a line," it said, "to let you know that this afternoon I went to the room where they dry the cocoons. They were talking about all kinds of things and I was enjoying it, but then I heard something about you that gave me a real turn, so I asked some more and the pinewood agent told me all about it. He said you never get any better at your service so you got chastised. I thanked him nicely. I felt I wanted to see you awfully, but I was so upset that I cried a lot on the way home. Anyway, you've been chastised twelve times already, that makes once every two years ever since I married you, and every time I've asked for time off from service here and gone to see how you were doing. I'm going to come again this time, I'll be there as soon as I can manage it. Not giving proper service is the same as being no good at your trade for someone in service like us, and if things go on this way we'll never be able to set up in our own house, so I do hope you'll do your best now."

I handed the letter back to the manservant.

He put it in his shirt pocket, utterly dispirited. The broad, deep creases that covered his face seemed to have gone rigid, as though they were the visible marks of his mental suffering. But he was not downcast for long.

"I don't suppose there's anything I can do about it. It's all the same anyway, isn't it?"

He got his saw from the back entrance and went off into the wood. He had certainly chosen a good way of effecting a change of mood. In the wood, I felt sure, he would find consolation in the task of tree felling. He had told me that when he went there, he would always manage to cut about one cord of firewood a day. He could saw straight through a tree two-foot-six in circumference without stopping once to rest.

From the direction of the wood there came the sound of a saw. The wood, known as Rokusa's wood, was a solid mass of conifers. Looking out from the window of my cottage, I found that the cottage stood on the edge of a cliff, and that I could look out onto Rokusa's wood almost directly beneath me. The sunlight reflected from the green of such dense trees forces one to narrow one's eyes to avoid the glare. A kind of heat rose up from the wood, yet at moments, depending on the way the wind blew, it struck my cheeks as almost cold. It was down there, in that wood, that the manservant was rasping away with his saw. One could imitate the sound by, for example, drawing a penholder back and forth over a poplin tablecloth; but it would be hard, I feel, to produce a sound that droned on so slowly and so unceasingly. The tree the manservant was cutting must be extraordinarily thick.

Mr. Tange came to see me in the cottage. He gazed out at one particular spot in Rokusa's wood and listened attentively to the sound of the saw, then asked me with a great air of secrecy:

"What was in the letter that came for our Ei?"

Something occurred to me. It occurred to me that he had decided that, having witnessed his unusual method of chastising his employee, I was no longer well disposed towards him.

"The letter was about cruel punishments," I said, with deliberate callousness.

"Dear me. That will mean that Otatsu will be coming again to give our Ei a piece of her mind. Yes, I'm sure she will. Well, let her come then!"

He leaned the upper half of his body out of the window and, looking down at Rokusa's wood, called out in a loud voice. It was as though he were calling, in the loudest voice that he could summon at his age, to the huge living creature that was the wood.

"Hello! Ei! If Otatsu is coming, you'd better clean up the house before she comes or she'll be telling you off again. Ei!"

From the depths of the wood came the reply, in a voice too small by far to be the wood's own:

"Let her come. Let her tell me off, I don't care!"

Again there came the sound of the saw.

Although I had asked him no question, Mr. Tange began to talk. He talked unceasingly, almost uncontrollably, about the past history of his manservant. Perhaps the old man felt awkward at having called to the forest so suddenly and in such a loud voice in my presence. A man faced suddenly and without warning with some embarrassing circumstance will become temporarily garrulous in an attempt to dispel his discomfiture.

"Otatsu will be fifty-three this year," began his monologue, "but she worries about her husband as though she were a newly married bride. It isn't as though she's ever had a household of her own since she and our Ei came together. Not only that, but the very day after she married him she said she was going into service and went off. So she's lived there all the time and hasn't come to see Ei so much as once a year. Nor do I believe our Ei has been to see her once. The fact is, when a man and woman in service get married after they are thirty and live apart, the man can hardly go and visit the woman at her place of work just to be with her. The mistress of the place would certainly guess that the man had just come so that he could be with the woman. And Otatsu herself, you see, couldn't find any excuse for coming to see Ei either, unless he was ill or in trouble. Not that I had the slightest idea of estranging them. That kind of thing would be wrong. As things are, I suppose, the pair of them are like a husband and wife who both have jobs away from home. Only in their case they don't have any home, anywhere, to go back to. The trouble is, you see, that our Ei had no family in the first place. How many years ago would it be, now . . .? It was when I was still young, around the time when I first started work at the village office, so it must be well over forty years by now. I was hulling rice in the back entrance, when a child suddenly appeared. He had his arms tucked inside his kimono, with the sleeves hanging loose, and his face showed he'd been crying. I had never seen him before in my life, so I asked him where he came from. 'I come from over there,' he said, pointing with his finger in the direction of the bridge across the valley. I expect he meant he'd come across the bridge before drifting into our house. I questioned him a lot, as gently as I could, but all he would say was 'I come from over there,' and that was as far as I got. I decided from the way he talked that he must be a stray from somewhere far away, so I gave him food and let him sleep a while in my bed, then I gave him something to help him on his way and sent him off. But no sooner did it begin to get dark than he turned up at our house again. It seemed he must be an orphan whose brain was affected. He sniffed continuously, and the discharge from his ears was so bad you couldn't go near him. Even so, we could hardly drive him away by force. I must have sent letters about him to thirty different village offices in all, but still I couldn't find where he had come from. The trouble was, you see, he knew nothing at all about himself even. Not a single thing, not even his own name. Dear me, how could anyone not feel pity for such a child.''

Lost in the memories of a full half century ago, Mr. Tange seemed suddenly seized by some strong emotion, for his eyes filled with tears. He gazed down at Rokusa's wood from the window,

106

his attention seemingly concentrated on the sound of the saw. A white veil of mist, rising from the valley, hung round about the wood.

"What nonsense," said Mr. Tange, with a small, mocking smile as though he found his own tears childish. "A lot of profitless memories. In those days, our family was in its prime; we had any number of family servants. I think you saw the small print on the back of the name card I once gave you, didn't you? The history of our family was explained in that. Our family was so well off that my revered teacher Rōro Sakatani actually wrote praising the pictures, calligraphy, and antiques in our possession. Ah, dear old Rōro, how the years do pass us by. . . . And here I am today, old and all alone. Ah, the sadness of it all. . . ."

As soon as he stopped speaking, Mr. Tange seemed to forget all about his lamentations for the past.

"The bath must be hot," he said to me. "Why don't you go and get in?"

Shocked and suspicious at the almost monastic life that the manservant had led, I demanded caustically of Mr. Tange why he had never given the couple their own household.

"Why, you see," he said almost proudly, "you might say it's their own private affair. Who can tell the motives behind other people's abstinences?"

He raised his eyes to the sky and for some while was lost in thought, then he heaved a sigh.

"And yet," he said, "should you ask what I've ever done for our Ei, the only thing, after all, may have been to give him the name Eisuke Tanishita. I can't help feeling that I've never really done anything else for the boy. I feel terrible when I think of it."

Leaving him there in the room, I got a shovel and bucket and went out. (I forgot to mention that I had come to the country in order to excavate the site of a kiln where they had once made a type of pottery known as Himetani ware. Dishes, tea jars, and other articles of Himetani ware are valued extremely highly, according to the histories of Japanese ceramics.)

As I was passing the wood, I saw the manservant sawing up a dead tree that had fallen to the ground. He was cutting it up into lengths of roughly six feet. On the ground nearby, a cluster of some heavy-leaved, lilylike plant had been crushed underfoot, and innumerable round, green seeds lay spilled on the ground. Hearing me coming, he paused in his work and greeted me as though we had not met since the previous day:

"Good day to you. Off somewhere, then?"

"Good day," I also said, observing the local custom, and went on my way.

The site of the kiln lay at the summit of a small hill. The hill was ringed by a sparse grove of oak trees; standing on the summit, you could look over the terraced fields from between their trunks. I seated myself on a mound of earth scattered with fragments that I had excavated, and looked at the crops, now nearing harvest-time. The heads of millet in one field bowed heavy with grain, near the peak of their growth, gleaming darkly beneath the direct rays of the sun. The last time I had passed by the field, I had seen a fieldmouse that had clambered up a stalk jump down in alarm at my footfall. In the cotton fields, stalks and leaves were brown and withered, and the pure white balls of cotton rested on calyxes that were equally brown. The balls were fluffy and full, and time and again I felt the urge to stretch out my hand and touch them.

My excavations threatened to make slow progress. After two weeks' efforts, I had dug up a single pitcher. It was decorated with an arabesque pattern in monochrome and was so massive that when I showed it to Mr. Tange and the manservant, the manservant said in disgust, "That's a terribly clumsy-looking saké bottle you've got there!"

The top of the hill was hot under the sun's rays, but it was cool beneath the oaks. Several vines climbed up the largest tree of all, and from them hung dozens of oval fruit, still green and solid.

Mr. Tange, the manservant, and I were sitting on the veranda after dinner, discussing a plan to release young carp in a backwater of the stream in the valley, when Otatsu arrived on her visit. She was a sturdily built woman, taller than her husband. In her hands she carried her belongings, wrapped in a straw bundle, and a semicircular bamboo basket containing chicks, which she had brought as a present. She put them down on the stone step below the veranda, then greeted Mr. Tange with heartfelt respect apparent in every feature of her face. The greetings began with a discussion of the merits of the climate, given in a quiet, rhythmical, singsong voice, and all the while she bowed so low with the upper half of her body that her hands reached down to her shins. To all this Mr. Tange responded with movements and words almost identical with those used by the woman. There was one passage in her greetings that ran:

"I've been thinking of coming to call on you for so long, but I never seem to get beyond thinking. I've kept telling myself that this time I was really going to come and see you, but I never seem to have found the time. . . ." To this Mr. Tange replied in what might be described as almost precisely the same terms. From this chanted dialogue, I gathered that Otatsu had left the place where she was in service at nine that morning, and had stopped to eat the meal she had brought with her on the bank of an irrigation pond at a place called Kureyama Valley, but had been so worried that she had left a good half of it uneaten. The worry was caused by the fact that her husband never got any better at his service. She had come, she said, to apologize for the error of his ways.

When she had finished greeting Mr. Tange, Otatsu turned to me. Mr. Tange introduced me as an amateur collector who had come from Tokyo to dig for pots, so she bowed courteously and said:

"Well now, such a long way for the gentleman to come."

With this preamble, she accorded me greetings almost identical with those she had given Mr. Tange. At a loss for the appropriate replies, I managed to tell her, in the intervals of her chant, how happy I was to report that the family's manservant was in the very best of health. I also told her with what self-sacrifice the family's manservant devoted himself to the service of his master.

Her greetings to me over, she glanced towards her husband and muttered with the utmost curtness:

"There's a good-for-nothing man for you!"

"What's good-for-nothing about me?" countered the manservant.

They said no more, but turned their backs on each other as though in silent reproach. Although this was the first time they had seen each other in two years, this unpretentious exchange seemed to satisfy them.

Mr. Tange gave his manservant instructions to show Otatsu to the bathroom, but the manservant did not obey. He was inspecting the contents of the present that stood on the stone step, muttering to himself as though in embarrassment, "What's the use of a stupid present like this?"

He got a bundle of straw and a wooden mallet out of the back entrance, placed the straw on a flat rock, and began to pound at it with the mallet. He probably felt that he was merely getting on with his evening work, but he wielded the mallet more forcefully than usual, even with a kind of abandon.

Otatsu went off to the bath alone, and reappeared almost immediately. She had merely washed her hands and face, but to Mr. Tange she said, "Thank you, the temperature was just right."

Mr. Tange, who was watching his servant at work, took a step or two forward.

"I never saw such an awkward devil," he muttered.

Otatsu must have been ashamed of the paltry present she had brought. Without consulting Mr. Tange, she rummaged about in the back entrance and the shed and produced a battered old wicker cage; she placed it at the foot of the persimmon tree and transferred her present to it. Alarmed by the sound of the manservant wielding his mallet, the six chicks, each like a ball of pure white cotton, rushed hither and thither raising faint cries of distress.

I went back to my cottage and gazed from the window at the

scene in the valley below. The moon was rising over the hills beyond—a large, red moon as it so often is these days, shining from the sky directly above, illuminating the upper layer of the mists that shrouded the valley below.

Yosaku the Settler

In the third month of the year 1694, the authorities of the Kobatake clan in the province of Bingo decided to open up for culti-
vation a stretch of open country known as Senyō Moor, and the
second and third sons of farmers in nearby villages were encouraged to come and settle on the land. Settlers would not only be
given subsidies but would be loaned hoes and seed grain as well.
As with other newly cultivated farmland, annual tributes were to
be waived for a period of three years.

The farmers of the clan knew that the soil on Senyō Moor was
poor. They also knew it as an uninhabited upland area where
crops were often ravaged by wild boars and hares. At first only the
very poor and those ostracised in their own villages would come
to settle there, but in time men from other provinces began to drift
in, men who had become paupers or, having lost their clan allegiance, were seeking new connections. A survey by an official of
the Kobatake clan, made in the twelfth month of the year 1696,
showed that on an upland area two or three miles square there
were now thirteen farmers' cottages. The total area under culti-
vation was some twenty-five acres.

To the southeast of Senyō Moor, on a low hill below the pass
over the mountains, there is a stone burial chamber dating from
distant antiquity. The tomb, of the type known nowadays as a
"horizontal-passage burial mound," has a narrow entrance lead-

ing to a chamber some ten square yards in area, with large stones forming its four walls and with three great stone slabs for its ceiling.

In the third month of the year 1697, a notice was set up at the entrance to the stone chamber, which said:

The following matters are strictly forbidden, on pain of severe punishment:

> *Entry into the chamber by any person whatsoever for unlawful purposes.*
> *Using the chamber for sleeping, sheltering from the rain, or gambling.*
> *Storing sweet potatoes in the chamber during the winter.*
> *Cutting nearby trees or plants.*
> *Tethering horses or cattle in the neighborhood.*

The Clan Office, Kobatake

First of the third month, 1697

As the items prohibited by the notice make clear, some of the new settlers had taken to gambling in the tomb, and others were using it for storing sweet potatoes.

Burial mounds are usually found in sunny places. They are warm in winter and, being made by piling up earth, are well drained. They are ideal for storing potatoes over the winter. Accordingly, three of the newly established farming households had chosen to use it jointly for storing their taros and yams, which they packed in rice husks in bamboo hampers and hid in a corner of the chamber. This fact came to light through the testimony of a farmer who was investigated by the clan office for having gambled in the tomb.

A record of the proceedings is to be found in the official records of the Kobatake clan office for the first half of the year 1697, which were kept until recently in an all but forgotten storehouse on the site of what was once the clan office. A year or two ago, I asked to see the documents concerning the affair of the burial chamber, and copied down the section relating to the questioning of the offender, modernizing the language as I went.

The farmer who did the gambling, a man called Yosaku, aged

thirty, was arrested on the eighteenth of the second month of 1697 on his way to worship at the Daihōji temple in Kobatake, the day being a festival dedicated to the celebrated Buddhist monk Hōnen. The title of "Saint Enkō" had been conferred on Hōnen by the Emperor on the eighteenth day of the previous month, and all the temples of the sect were holding great services to celebrate the honor. Yosaku was stopped for questioning by an official of this clan office on account of a silver pipe he had in his mouth, which was held to be inappropriate to his station in life.

The officials who questioned Yosaku at the clan office were Mitarō Kosaka and Kimpyōe Mori. They were joined on the twenty-second of the second month by Shume Miya, who took over as chief investigator. In addition to these, there were four guards in attendance.

There was one scribe at first, and three from the twenty-second of the second month. The records of the examination for the nineteenth of the second month are as follows:

Question: Your name is Yosaku, I believe. Your age is thirty, and you were born in Takaya village, in the district of Shitsuki in the province of Bitchū. Your aunt by marriage being resident in the village of Kobatake of the Kobatake clan, you received official permission to settle on Senyō Moor and start a farm through the good offices of your aunt. Are these facts correct?
Answer: They are correct, your honor.
Q. On the occasion of the service at the Daihōji temple, you were stopped for questioning by an official agent concerning a silver pipe of a quality unsuited to your station, and in the course of an immediate inquiry you proved, I believe, to have this purse in your possession. Is that so?
A. It is so, your honor.
Q. The purse in question would seem to be a souvenir of a visit to the Grand Shrines of Ise. But it is new, as though it had been purchased recently. Who brought it back for you from Ise?
A. I had it from an acquaintance living nearby, your honor.

115

Q. I am not convinced by your answer. Visits to the Grand Shrines have become too popular and ostentatious in recent years, and the clan office permitted no farmers to make the pilgrimage to Ise either last year or the year before. There is not a single farmer in this clan who visited the shrines other than clandestinely. Nor did any farmer among the new settlers at Senyō Moor apply for permission to make a pilgrimage to Ise. What was the name of this neighbor who you say gave you the purse, then? Scoundrel! Take care what you say!

A. Certainly, your honor. I'll tell the truth. I got it from a stranger from other parts.

Q. No doubt you took strangers in for gambling and received this as your share of the proceeds. You ran a gambling den in defiance of the law, is that not so? We shall proceed to your cottage, then, for a thorough search. Lead the way!

A. Your worship—please listen. I didn't use my cottage as a gambling den. We used the burial chamber below the pass.

Q. Unspeakable villain! Who gave you permission to use the chamber? The burial chamber below the pass, along with the imperial tomb at Hiba, is one of the two most hallowed tombs in this area, as sacrosanct as the inner sanctuary in a Shinto shrine or the casket housing the holy image in a Buddhist temple. Nobody is supposed to have set foot in it since its consecration. Who incited you to enter the chamber? Give us his name!

A. I wasn't incited by anybody, your worship. Most of the new farmers on Senyō Moor keep sweet potatoes in the tomb.

Q. Enough! How dare you use that sacred tomb as a substitute for a potato jar! Even to mention such a thing is sacrilege. But do you have proof of all this?

A. Only the other day I was up there in the tomb with a stranger from other parts. At that time, there were hampers holding taros, yams, and sweet potatoes.

Q. A pretty story, indeed! If it is not false, tell us more details of these hampers.

A. Certainly, your honor. The yams were in a hamper filled with

116

rice husks. There were four of these hampers. I tried picking one up with both hands, and I'd say at a rough guess there were fifty pounds in one basket. There must have been about two hundred pounds altogether.

Q. Well said. With seed yams, one farmer's family would do with forty-two pounds. If there were some two hundred pounds, four or five families must be keeping theirs there together.

A. That's right, your honor. By now, we settler farmers have eaten all our potatoes except the seed ones. If you keep them nearby, you end up eating the lot, seed potatoes included. Farmers are a greedy lot, you see. I expect they keep them in the tomb so that they're out of reach. I assure you, your honor, that no disrespect was meant for this imperial tomb or whatever you called it.

Q. Enough! Do you suggest it is no disrespect to gamble in an imperial tomb? You try to blame your own misdeeds on others, and you quibble with words. What do you take the clan office for, impertinent creature! That is all for today. You may go back to your cell."

The day's investigation was cut short at this point, and Mitarō Kosaka, the examining official, immediately purified himself in cold water and set off for the tomb below the pass with two retainers and the priest from a Shinto shrine. Although he was an official personage, he was about to enter a sacred spot, and he commanded the priest to pacify the local spirits before they entered the chamber.

The priest offered up a prayer, then waved a wand with white paper streamers at one end, chanting as he did so, "Wrath of the hills, away, away! Wrath from the earth's depths, away, away! The word of the gods shall never lie. Wrath of the hills, away, away. . . ."

Ordering a retainer to light a lantern he had ready, Mitarō went into the stone chamber, leaving the priest alone outside. The entrance was small and the interior in darkness. They had to rely solely on the light of the paper lantern with "On Official Service"

117

inscribed on it that the retainer held up for them, but they soon discovered the hampers, lined up along the stone wall: four with taros packed in rick husks, two containing yams, and three with sweet potatoes.

One of the retainers lifted a hamper of taros with both hands and said:

"A good fifty pounds, your honor."

"Hold up the lantern to give more light."

Mitarō made him expose the flame of the candle inside; then, with a writing brush that he took from a container tucked in the front of his kimono, and a piece of handmade paper, he drew a diagram showing the position of the hampers and added a brief verbal explanation.

"There's a potato here," said one of the retainers.

Bringing the light closer, they found the chewed remains of a taro lying in a pile on the stone floor. Congealed on the stone nearby was some wax that had dropped from a candle.

The accounts of the interior of the stone chamber, as well as the following record of the interrogation, are from the clan's official record. The clan office in Kobatake seems to have suspected from the start that Yosaku was concealing some other, more serious crime. Everything concerning Yosaku was duly noted down, major and minor matters alike. It is just possible, also, that an informer had already told them of Yosaku's earlier offenses, and that they merely used the silver pipe as a pretext for arresting him.

The fief of Kobatake in the province of Bingo belonged to the Nakatsu clan in Kyushu, from which it was geographically separated. All incidents occurring within its territory that related to other clans were investigated with particular care so as to avoid trouble later. It seems most likely that the fact that Yosaku had done wrong in other provinces was passed on secretly by some informer.

On the twentieth of the second month, two days before the second interrogation of Yosaku, the clan officials left him shut up in jail and went to search his hovel. When they asked Yosaku's wife her name and age, she went quite stiff, and stayed motionless by the water jar until the officials left.

The house, like those of other farmers in the neighborhood, consisted of a dirt-floored section some ten square yards in area; a room of the same size with a boarded floor covered with straw matting, separated from the dirt-floored section by neither sliding doors nor any other partition; and a floored space of some three square yards for keeping the bedding, the wicker baskets for holding clothes, and so on. The officials searched the latter thoroughly, but there was nothing suspicious.

"Where's your Buddhist altar?" asked the official.

"We don't have one yet," said the wife.

"Where's the Shinto altar?" the official asked.

"We don't have one yet," she replied.

The retainers accompanying the official ripped up the mats in the room. The floor underneath, which was made of rows of uncut bamboo and was full of cracks, offered little scope for hiding purses or other valuables.

"Well, Mrs. Yosaku, where does Yosaku usually keep his money?" asked the official.

"There." She pointed to a shelf suspended from the ceiling by stout ropes. "In the black cabinet on the shelf." She was quite a cooperative woman.

On the hanging shelf there stood two cabinets, one black, the other light brown. The official's retainers took down the black cabinet, opened it, and, together with a small tub containing bean paste, a bowl, and other domestic articles, took out a purse.

"You there, woman—come and watch this."

He called her, but she remained rooted to the spot, so he went and opened the purse beside her. There were three or four grains of gold, and two cancelled IOU's. One of the latter was for a trifling sum and raised no comment, but the other was for twelve *ryō*. It showed that he had borrowed it four years ago, in the first month of the year 1693, from a man called Kampachi of Takaya village in the province of Bitchū, and had returned the whole sum in the second month of the same year. That someone with the status of an impoverished farmer should have borrowed a sum as large as twelve *ryō* and repaid it within a month was highly suspicious. Moreover, there was also a comma-shaped jewel of jade in the purse.

The official interrogated Yosaku's wife on the spot. The exchange was noted down in writing by one of the retainers.

It is transcribed in the official record of the clan as follows:

On the twentieth of the second month, at the home of Yosaku in the newly settled village, Kimpyōe Mori conducted a cross-examination of Yosaku's wife.

Yosaku's wife, born in Takaya village, province of Bitchū; name Kishi; age 27.

Question: How long have you been married to Yosaku?
Answer: This is the fourth year.
Q. Do you remember this IOU? For what purpose did Yosaku need to borrow such a large sum as twelve *ryō*?
A. Yes, I remember the IOU, your honor. Four of five years ago Yosaku bought me out of the Izutsu-ya in the gay quarters at Kannabe. He made a point of showing it to me then.
Q. How did you come to be friendly with Yosaku when you were working at the Izutsu-ya? A poor farmer like Yosaku could hardly afford to become a regular patron of yours.
A. I'd known Yosaku ever since I was small. As he was poor he had to borrow the money to buy me out.
Q. Can you read? If you can, look at this figure. Twelve *ryō*. Look at the date. He borrowed it on the fifteenth of the first month of 1693, and returned it on the tenth of the next month. The creditor, a man called Kampachi, wrote it and stamped it with his seal. How did he get the money to return it—did he sell some paddies or something?
A. He gave Kampachi three jewels and a Chinese mirror instead.
Q. Who is this Kampachi?

A. He's an important man who lives in Kannabe. He often used to come to the Izutsu-ya. He was a regular patron of Otane, who was a kind of elder sister to me there.

Q. Then it was through this Otane that Yosaku borrowed money from Kampachi?

A. Yes, your honor. I met Yosaku—I'd known him as a child—one night at a festival while I was in service at the Izutsu-ya. I told him I didn't like being in service, and said I'd be his wife if he'd take me away. Yosaku said he hadn't any money but he had some green jewels that were worth a lot. So I told Otane, and she spoke to Kampachi for me.

Q. Well said. You're a sensible woman. Then where did Yosaku say he got the green jewels?

A. He said he'd been to visit the Grand Shrines of Ise on the quiet. On the way back, someone persuaded him to take a job as a laborer, helping clear away the ruins of the great fire in Kyoto. He worked dragging the riverbed too, and it was while he was there that he found the green jewels and the mirror in the river.

Q. You mean, that's what Yosaku told you. Is that right?

A. That's right, your honor.

The general picture was clear by now. The clan office brought in an official called Shume Miya, a man of great perception, in order to carry out a thorough investigation.

From the twenty-second of the second month, Miya became chief examiner in the investigation of Yosaku. The day before, he set off on horseback to visit Kampachi's home in Kannabe, and came back to Kobatake on the morning of the twenty-second. The treasure that Kampachi had received from Yosaku as security consisted of three curved jewels in jade and an old Chinese mirror.

Miya installed himself in the most important seat and Kimpyōe Mori, in the seat next to him, began the proceedings by reading to Yosaku, from a document he held in front of him, the testimony of his wife Kishi. "Is this true?" he concluded.

"It is true, your honor," Yosaku replied.

At this point his wife Kishi was taken away to another room.

When Miya began his inquiry, Yosaku confessed with almost disappointing alacrity. He still did not seem to realize the enormity of the crime he had committed. The green stones had not been picked up in the River Kamo at Kyoto but acquired in the province of Yamato. He had visited the Grand Shrines of Ise, then, hearing that laborers were being recruited to help clear up after the great fire, had gone to Kyoto to earn some money. But he had gambled away all he earned, and in a kind of despair had set off for the province of Yamato, begging as he went. He had picked up two companions on the way. Carried away by their talk, he had agreed to join them in opening up a burial chamber and sharing its treasures among the three of them.

"I will tell your honor. The place was far bigger than the stone chamber below the pass at Senyō Moor. It was really magnificent. Even the entrance had stone steps going up to it."

This testimony of Yosaku's caused a sudden stir among the officials present. One has only to glance at the official record today to tell that the chief investigator, Shume Miya, was flurried. He plied Yosaku with questions in rapid succession.

Question: What is the name of the tomb where the stone chamber was? How did the entrance look? What shape was the mound—round or like a gourd? It may have been only another burial chamber, but any burial chamber in the area of the capital is an extraordinarily hallowed spot. First tell us the shape of the hill. Round, or gourd-shaped?

Answer: It was night, and I couldn't make out the shape of the outside, your honor. It seems it was a small, gently rounded hill, though. Two days running, after it got dark, we went and tried to force open the stone door at the entrance, but it wasn't till the third night, your honor, that we managed it.

Q. Misguided wretch! I can hardly imagine, even so, that you dared set foot in the inner sanctuary. How was the stone portal at the entrance made? Tell us in detail.

A. As far as I could tell in the light from the east just before dawn, I think the stone door faced south. There was a dried-up ditch all round the hill, and in it there were longish stones set in a kind of zigzag pattern, pointing towards the stone door.

Q. That would be a stone bridge, lying where it had collapsed. A dried-up ditch, you say. . . . Long ago, I suppose, it would have been a moat full of water. What is the name of the burial mound, then?

A. I'm afraid I didn't ask the name, your honor. The only thing the boss said was that we were going to open up a burial chamber. It was way out in the country, a good five miles off the main road leading from the province of Yamashiro to the province of Yamato. In a village with three big horse-chestnut trees behind a water mill at the side of the road.

Q. What a fool the man is! He steals the treasures without knowing the name of the tomb he broke open or even that he's guilty of an unheard-of act of treason. You did not, of course, go right into the inner sanctuary to rob it? I imagine your loot was located in the narrow passageway leading from the entrance. Tell us everything now, honestly and without prevarication.

A. I will tell you, your honor. The treasures were in a big chamber leading off the end of the narrow passageway. We lit three candles, and we could see the ceiling was about six feet high. The chamber was a good twelve or thirteen feet deep and about ten feet across.

Q. *That* was the inner shrine. That, you should know, is the most sacrosanct spot of all. Tell us in detail, and with proper reverence, what the inner sanctuary was like.

A. The stone chamber—this inner sanctuary as you call it—had gilded pillars on all four sides, with gilded panel doors. In the middle of the chamber there was a stone thing like a rather long water tank full of what looked like bits of old reins and bridles, all dried up and moldy. There was one more like it. The boss said that they were coffins and I wasn't to touch, but he felt down to the bottom of them all the same and fetched out some jewels. On the right of the stone thing, there was a box about a foot square done in openwork. The boss forced the lid open with his dagger, and there was a round china pot in it full of gold dust. Besides that, there were bits of wood like a torch used for kindling, done up in a bundle with gold thread. The boss said the bundle was aromatic wood, and stuck it in the front of his kimono. He wrapped the pot of gold dust up in a cloth; he said he'd divide it up among us later. It held about five *gō* and it was full, but he kept it all for himself. He only gave me one small bit of the perfumed wood, too. He was a mean devil, the boss. . . .

Q. The fragrant wood would have been heart of aloes or something similar, for certain. Aloes wood, tied with a golden cord—what could be more elegant? And what else did you steal from the openwork box?

A. Apart from that, there was an inkstone and a block of solid ink. Oh yes, and a round thing like an openwork ball. The ink was shaped like a rhododendron leaf—"Chinese ink," the boss said it was called. He kept that for himself, too. And there was a shallow gilded tray with a silver jug rusted all black on it, and a cup made of something like crystal. In the same tray there was a thing like a string of prayer beads, made of jewels on a gold thread, and something like a little wind-bell done in gold. I think there were all kinds of other out-of-the-way things too, but I can only remember what the boss took. I forget completely what the other man with me had for his share. At any rate, when we left the chamber we went a long way round by the road over the mountains and came out on the highway, then we hid ourselves for a while in a little temple. The monk there might have been a friend of the boss's or he might not, it's difficult to say. Anyway, we had a good sleep in the priest's quarters. There's not much more to tell. I left the others and traveled alone back to Takaya village in Bitchū.

Q. Which of the objects stolen from the stone chamber did you receive as your share?

A. My share—I'm not likely to forget—was four green jewels, seven red jewels, a piece of metalwork like a teapot stand, and a piece of the fragrant wood. The boss made a great fuss about the thing like a teapot stand when he gave it to me. He said it was a mirror from China, worth a hundred *ryō*. But what he said was lies. On the way to Takaya, I had myself quite a good time in Osaka, and I took the mirror to a secondhand shop to try and sell it. But they told me that though it might be Chinese it was poor workmanship and only worth about one *ryō*. So I got by with the fragrant wood.

Q. So the old Chinese mirror and three of the green jewels are what you gave to Kampachi in Kannabe as security for the twelve *ryō*. The remaining stone you put away in the purse. What about the fragrant wood—what do you mean when you say you "got by with it"?

A. On my way back to Takaya, I presented it to the Shinshū temple at Okayama, and they gave me a night's lodging. I got four or five grains of gold as well, as a special reward. That's the truth your honor, every word of it.

Q. What you say makes everything more or less clear. I will tell you something, though. You should know that the crime of breaking open an imperial tomb as you have done is far more serious than you might think.

A. Yes, your honor.

Q. There are various degrees in the crimes committed by human beings. Under the T'ang code, they were classified into ten categories, in our country into nine. They are: insurrection, treason, revolt, evildoing, immorality, lèse-majesté, disloyalty, filial disobedience, and impropriety. But the crime of breaking open an imperial tomb is of a seriousness equivalent to all of these rolled into one. For this reason, it seems that very few persons have ever violated imperial tombs. Such a criminal only appears, they say, once in two or even three centuries, and then only in times of moral depravity. Your wrongdoing is of an enormity seen only once in two or three hundred years!

A. Yes, your honor.

Q. Today, however, it happens that Shinshin Maeda, the great scholar of our classical literature, called at the clan office as he was passing through on a journey. When I told the master of your crime, he was very curious about such an unusual offence. "I've searched all over the country," he told me, "but I've found almost no one who has seen the inside of an imperial tomb with his own eyes. I would like—with the official permission of the clan office and the assent of the criminal—to meet the criminal at his convenience." That is what the master said. Are you ready to meet him and tell him the secrets of the interior of the tomb? The master is a great authority on the culture of our nation. What better chance for you to give a little grace to your last days?

A. Your honor—I am an uncouth sort of person. I will do as you direct me. I am a criminal, so it is not for me to decide.

Q. Listen carefully. The master Maeda also had this to say. In all the countless books preserved since ancient times, there are very few accounts of the violation of an imperial tomb. One such account, it seems, occurs in the diary of Lord Teika Fujiwara. It appears from his account that in the fourth month of the year 1234, in the reign of the Emperor Shijō, a thief violated the imperial tomb near the Tachibana temple in Yamato province and stole the imperial treasures. The tomb in question houses the remains of the Emperor Temmu and the Empress Jitō, and is known as the Abuki Mausoleum. There is another account of the thief who broke into this tomb in an ancient work called the "Annals of the Imperial Tomb at Abuki." However, it seems that there is little detail concerning the stone chamber inside the tomb. There are no other old records dealing with imperial tombs, and the scholars of national learning have all been complaining of this lack. And now, here are you, who have seen the interior of the inner chamber of an imperial tomb with your own eyes—and by the light of three candles, too. "What a splendid opportunity," Master Maeda was saying. If you meet the master, you had better calm your mind and tell him all the details you can. This is something that will further the study of our national culture.

A. Your honor, it just came back to me—in the tomb we opened

126

there was something else, a long stone chest on legs. When we opened the lid, we found a lot of things they use in wars—some stuff like chain mail, and a long spearhead, and a long sword with gold work on it. It was all eaten away with rust.

Q. You made off with the gold work as well, I suppose?

A. No, the boss hauled all the stuff out of the chest and threw it in a pile in a corner of the chamber. The boss said that one day when his time comes, he'd come back to the burial chamber and lay himself to eternal rest in the stone chest there. He said people in days to come would see his bones and think he was buried there when the chamber was made.

Q. Insolent, outrageous evildoer that he is! However, the investigation will be suspended for today at this point. When you get back to your cell, you had better make sure that you remember the inside of the chamber as clearly as possible.

The official record shows that the examination of Yosaku continued until the end of the second month, but the account of it is extremely brief. "Examining officer Shume Miya: investigation of Yosaku," is all it says. In all probability, he was made to confess the names of the others who gambled with him in the stone chamber below the pass. Nothing at all is recorded as to whether Yosaku did in fact meet the great classical scholar, Shinshin Maeda. There is no mention, even, of the all-important question of the verdict passed on Yosaku.

The farmers who kept their sweet potatoes in the tomb were also, all five of them, summoned for questioning. The account is in the official record. "However ignorant you may be," an official is recorded as reprimanding them, "you must know how outrageous it is to store potatoes in the tomb of a noble person. Yours is a serious crime!"

According to the official record for the first half of the next year but one, the farmers of the newly settled village on Senyō Moor, all of them, to a man, had taken flight. Their crops had been dealt heavy blows by the snows of the previous winter and by the summer drought; they had been unable to pay the annual tribute that should have commenced the previous year, and the whole village, by common consent, had taken to its heels one night. The report made by the official who went to search their cottages, commenting on the completely bare state in which he had found them, says, "There was nothing there in the first place."

Savan on the Roof

For certain, some wanton hunter or mischievous marksman had taken a shot at it. I found it, a wild goose, lying in pain on the bank of a swamp. Its left wing was wet with its own blood, and it was flapping its good wing in vain, sending out cries of distress over the densely growing waterweed of the marshland.

Treading softly, I crept up to the wounded goose and picked it up in both hands. The warmth of the bird's feathers and body transmitted itself to my hands, and the unexpected weight came as a solace to my weary mind. I determined that I would make the bird better, and took it home, cradling it in my hands. I fastened the shutters tightly in my room, and set about treating its wound beneath the light of a five-candle-power electric lamp.

But a wild goose, it seems, can see even in a dim light, and it kicked over the metal bowl of carbolic acid and the bottle of iodoform, hindering my attempts to operate on it. So—and I admit it was a rather drastic measure—I bound its legs with thread, pressed its right wing against its body as it struggled, and gripped its long, thin neck between my knees.

"Stay still, won't you!" I scolded.

But still it insisted on sadly misinterpreting my good intentions, and steadily, all through my treatment, I could hear from between my knees the cry that wild geese give as they wing across the sky late on autumn nights.

Even after I had finished attending to it, I left it tied up until the wounds should stop bleeding; otherwise, it might have thrown itself about the room and got dirt in them.

I was worried about the results of my treatment. Having no surgical instruments, I used the blade from a pencil sharpener to gouge out the four pellets, then washed the wound with carbolic acid and poured iodoform on it. Of six pellets that had entered the flesh of the wing from the underside, two had gone right through and come out at the top. I imagine that the man who shot at it had pulled the trigger of his gun as he saw the goose rising up into the sky. The stricken goose would have come falling diagonally from the sky into the waterweeds, where it had doubtless hoped to rest until the pain of its wound got better. It was then that I had come by, strolling along the banks of the marsh in a mood of quite indescribable depression.

Leaving the goose tied up in the center of the room, I went into the next room to wash the smell of carbolic off my hands and prepare some food to give to the bird. But I found that I had tired myself out, and, deciding to catch a little sleep, I propped myself up against the brazier. This kind of nap is often unexpectedly protracted; sometimes it happens that one does not wake up until late at night.

It was, in fact, around midnight that I awoke, startled by the raucous cry of a goose. The wounded bird in the next room had given three short, shrill calls. Stepping quietly, I went and peered through a gap in the sliding doors. With its legs and wings still bound, the wild goose was stretching its neck towards the five-candle-power electric lamp as though about to cry out again. In all probability, the injured bird had mistaken the light of the lamp for the moon as it looks in the small hours.

When the goose's wounds had completely healed, I clipped the feathers of both wings so that I could let it run free in the garden. It seemed to be very tame; whenever I went out, it would follow me as far as the gate, and late at night would walk around the house like a dog that is faithful to its master. I gave the goose the name Savan, and would take him with me when I went for walks along country paths or down to the swamp.

"Savan! Savan!" I would call. And Savan would come walking after me on sleepy legs.

The marshy land was dressed for early summer. Waterweeds almost as high as myself grew thickly along the bank, their broad leaves and white flowers spreading in profusion over the surface of the water. Somehow, Savan seemed to take a fancy to this swamp. Slipping into the water, he would beat his short wings and shake his tail, refusing to come out, however often I called him, until he was tired of his bath. It was my habit at such times to sprawl in the clumps of grass and give myself up to my own thoughts. And so I might, for I had not come to the swamp to keep an eye on Savan while he bathed but to drive away the cares that beset my own mind.

Not content with swimming on the water, Savan also liked to dive beneath the surface. At times, he would even stay hidden under the surface. Fortunately, however, the water is clear in this swamp and I could see him grubbing for food below.

Wild geese do not really like daylight and the warmth of the sun. Whenever I left him to his own devices he would crouch all day beneath the corridor, dozing. But at night (I always shut the garden gate so that he could not run away) he would be quite lively and try to make holes in the hedge or jump over the gate.

It was one day when summer was past and autumn already at hand that it happened. It was late at night, after a fierce, chill wind had blown itself out. I was in my cotton night kimono with a padded jacket draped over my shoulders, holding over the glowing charcoal of the brazier a pair of socks, washed by myself that afternoon, that were still damp. At times such as these, one is apt to dwell on personal affairs or to stick one's hands in one's pockets and tell oneself idly that one will get up early the next morning. Occasionally, one does not even notice that the socks drying over the fire are beginning to smell scorched. . . . But just then, I heard Savan give a shrill cry, a cry that transformed the late night quiet

131

into an awe-inspiring clamor; something, for sure, had happened outside to set Savan's nerves on edge.

I opened the window.

"Savan! Stop that noise!"

But Savan's cries did not stop. In the cluster of trees outside the window, each twig was still loaded with rain. The eaves were dewed with drops; to touch them would have brought the drops showering down in hundreds. Yet the sky by now was quite clear; it was a moonlit night.

I climbed over the windowsill and went outside. There, on the very top of my roof, stood Savan, stretching his long neck high up towards the sky, calling in the loudest voice he could summon. In the sky, in the direction towards which he stretched his neck, the moon was shining, reddish-tinged and misshapen as it so often is when it rises late at night. And high up in the sky, crossing the moon from left to right, three wild geese were flying into the distance. I realized what was happening. The three geese aloft and Savan on the roof were calling to each other with all their might. Savan would give three short cries, and one of the geese would echo them back. They must be saying something to each other. Savan, I felt sure, was crying to his three comrades, "Take me with you!"

I interrupted his cries, afraid he might run away. "Savan! Come down from the roof!"

But unlike his usual self, Savan ignored my command and went on calling desperately after the other three wild geese. I tried whistling to him and beckoning to him with both hands, till in the end I could stand it no longer and was obliged to get a stick and beat the boughs of the trees in the garden.

"Savan!" I shouted. "It's dangerous up there so high. Come down, quickly! Savan—come down, now, as I tell you!"

But Savan made no move to come down from the summit of the roof until his fellows had vanished from both sight and hearing. Anyone who had seen him then would surely have been reminded of an aged philosopher, banished to a distant, lonely island, gazing after the first vessel in ten years to pass by offshore.

132

To stop Savan from jumping up onto the roof or anywhere else again, I should have tied a string to his leg and fastened the other end to a post. But I refrained from anything so drastic. It was quite incredible to me that he should betray my affection and go off to distant parts. I had clipped the feathers of his wings so short that to clip them further would have injured him. I did not like to treat him too harshly.

So all I did, the next day, was to scold him roundly.

"Savan! You wouldn't run away, would you? You must give up any such ungrateful idea."

I gave him enough food to last three days and more.

It had become a habit for Savan to climb onto the roof, where, without fail, he would cry out in a shrill voice. He invariably chose bright moonlit nights, and the late hours. At such times, propping my elbows on the table or lying late in bed at night, I would strain to hear the cries of the geese passing across the night skies, echoing Savan's calls as they went. Theirs were the faintest of distant cries, too faint, almost, to be audible. If one chose to, one might have heard them as a sigh wrung from the late hour itself in its solitude; which would have meant, I suppose, that Savan was conversing with the sighing of the night.

One night, Savan cried still more shrilly than usual. It was almost a lamentation. But since I knew that his visits to the roof were the only times when he would not obey my commands, I made no move to go out and see what was up. I sat at my desk and prayed that his cries would cease soon, and told myself that from tomorrow I would have to give up clipping his wings so as to give him the freedom to fly away. After I got into bed, I pulled the quilts up as far as my forehead to help me go to sleep, much as a child does in an attempt to shut out the howling of the wind and the rain. As a result, I could no longer hear Savan's lamentation, but the image of Savan standing on the roof crying up to the sky refused to leave me. And so, since the Savan of my imagination also cried out shrilly, I suffered just the same.

I made up my mind. The next morning, I would put some medicine on Savan's wings to make the feathers grow fast. The fresh new feathers would allow him to soar up into the sky to his heart's content. Should I be seized by an old-fashioned impulse, I might even fasten a tin ring round his leg. And on it, I would engrave in small letters: "Fly, Savan! Fly high and happy, into the moonlit sky!"

The next day, I realized that Savan was not about.

"Savan! Where are you, Savan!"

A sense of panic seized me. He was nowhere to be seen, neither under the corridor nor up on the roof. On the iron sheeting projecting below the eaves, I found a single breast feather that clearly belonged to Savan. It stirred in the morning breeze, caught in the join between two pieces of iron. I hurried to the swamp to look.

He did not seem to be there either. By now the tall weeds along the bank had formed spikes at the tips of their stalks, and their fluffy seeds scattered over my shoulders and hat.

"Savan! Are you there, Savan? Come out if you are! Please, Savan! Show yourself. . . ."

Beneath the water, I could see the rotting leaves of plants, lying on the bed of the swamp: Savan was certainly not there, either. For sure, I told myself, he had set off on his seasonal travels, borne up on the wings of his comrades.